THE
CASSOWARY

JAMES SABATA

THE CASSOWARY

First Trade Paperback Edition November 2020

Cover Design © 2020 ELDERLEMON DESIGN
Interior Art © 2020 EVIL CRIMMY

Text set in Libre Baskerville

DESIGNED BY J. PATRICK MCCORD

ISBN–13:9798554466939

Visit
www.JamesSabata.com
for more information on this and other great works.

Dedicated to anyone who has worked to make the days of quarantine and COVID–19 a little more bearable for anyone else, particularly a group of horror writers on Twitter who brought this "series" to life and helped me find a light in these dark times.

This book is further dedicated to the many organizations involved with The Cassowary Recovery Team, who work tirelessly to help preserve the cassowary's dwindling environment and help us learn more about these beautiful, secretive birds. Proceeds from this book will go to them.

To learn more, visit
HTTP://CassowaryRecoveryTeam.org

This book was written for charity with proceeds from profits going to different organizations that care for cassowaries. THE CASSOWARY RECOVERY TEAM is a group of organizations working together to implement a Recovery Plan for the Southern Cassowary. Their aim is to protect cassowaries, habitats, and corridors from threats through better planning, monitoring, and community involvement.

The CRT plays an important role in ensuring community, government and research activities undertaken in support of cassowary conservation are aligned and coordinated, and that knowledge is shared as a basis for informed action. An underlying principle of the recovery team is that all members will benefit from their participation through gaining knowledge and achieving efficiencies in plan implementation. Their continued efforts provide a boost to the odds of survival of the cassowary.

Your purchase of this book does as well.

THE PECKING ORDER

Chapter One	13
Chapter Two	17
Chapter Three	25
Chapter Four	31
Chapter Five	39
Chapter Six	47
Chapter Seven	55
Chapter Eight	65
Chapter Nine	74
Chapter Ten	81
Chapter Eleven	87
Chapter Twelve	95
Chapter Thirteen	103
Chapter Fourteen	111
Chapter Fifteen	119
Chapter Sixteen	127
Chapter Seventeen	135
Chapter Eighteen	143
Chapter Nineteen	155

It started with the crazy headline: "Australian Town Terrorized by Muscular Kangaroo Attacking People and Eating Gardens." Pretty quickly, a group of authors on Twitter were sharing it, talking about how it sounded like something Alan Baxter (the only Australian author in the conversation) would write.

Kealan Patrick Burke cranked out an amazing mock cover. Alan made some changes to it and wrote the book. *The Roo* went on to become my personal favorite thing I read in 2020.

More authors decided to join in on the creature feature fun and Kealan was kind enough to create the covers for our books as long as the proceeds were going to charity. Everyone agreed to pick an animal indigenous to where they live and write their own creature feature. Stephanie Rabig created *Playing Possum*. Sean Seebach brought us *The Buck Stops Here.*

Wait. Did I say everyone?

One person[1] just got super excited and misread everything and somehow thought we were supposed to use Australian animals. "What an easy choice!" I screamed to no one in particular. I cranked out a quick pitch to do The Cassowary. Kealan shot back the cover of the book you are reading now.

I realized my mistake, panicked, and emailed everyone back, "Oh. It's supposed to be an animal where I live?" I pitched a different story and explained that I am kind of an idiot who only half reads things sometimes. Then came the response, "Oh, no. You are doing *The Cassowary*. That's amazing."

And that's how some guy in Phoenix, AZ, the literal antithesis of the rainforest habitat a cassowary needs to survive, ended up writing this book. I hope you enjoy it as much as I enjoyed creating it.

---

1. It was me

CHAPTER ONE

Michael Flanders turned the key in the gate of the Toscano Wildlife Preserve just before the midnight hour. He locked the gate behind him and inhaled the unseasonable chill in the air. Arizona didn't get many nights like this and he knew not to waste this one.

He glanced into the dark gift shop as he passed, his own reflection the only thing out of place. Moving at a steady pace through the zoo, Michael greeted each animal as he passed their enclosures. He carried no flashlight, relying solely on the soft glow of endless pathway lights. After twenty-four years, he knew the meandering dirt driveways, wooden walkways, and paved paths around the exhibits better than his own home in many respects.

Michael stopped halfway across the wooden bridge leading to the kangaroo exhibit. His hand pushed deep into his pocket; his fingers flailing around inside until they found a quarter. He turned the coin in his hand before placing it into the red deluxe fish food vending machine. Turning the handle reminded him of the gumball machines of his youth. The dusty brown pellets falling into his hand weren't nearly as awe inspiring as those shiny spheres of flavored gum had once been.

Michael watched the pellets fall from his palm and cascade to the water; the surface almost instantly replaced with the koi below. Mouths opened and closed quickly, whether they found food or not.

Michael watched the fish feast for several minutes, listening to the ambient sounds playing over the speakers scattered throughout the zoo.

The light crunch of his soles against the dirt reminded Michael he was alone in the zoo; at least as far as humans were concerned. He rounded the path near the Crested Screamer, awaiting the bird's loud double−noted trumpet call, but none came.

The animal he had come to see that night came into view. The cassowary faced away from him, but as Michael called, "Good morning, Cassie." The large bird crouched down in a brooding pose, much like she would have if she was preparing to mate. Her eyes were closed.

Michael admired the keratinous casque on her head, as he had since she had begun growing it: The Queen's Crown, as he called it.

Michael smiled. "Glad you're feeling better! I was getting worried about you, girl!" He turned away, before calling back, "I'm gonna go fix you a snack. I'll be back shortly."

As Michael turned his back, the 150−pound bird rose, exposing her long, powerful reptilian−like legs.

Her eyes shot open. A pink light shone from her pupils so brightly it illuminated the enclosure, reflecting even in her coat of iridescent black feathers. Her beak clapped several times in quick succession. A low grumble filled the air around her as she awaited her prey.

One hand carried a bag of plums and a small knife to pit them. The other popped the lock. Michael pulled the door and stepped into the small area before the next security door; the one with the yellow diamond shaped sign that read, "DANGEROUS BIRD. DO NOT ENTER WITHOUT KEEPER."

Michael had not stepped foot in the actual

cassowary pen while the animal was there since she was a very young bird. When she chose to go into the side area and he knew it was secured, he would go in and clean the pen some mornings or late afternoons. Still he would never dream of entering the pen at night, even if some of the other keepers had in the past.

"They usually only attack when they're provoked; but the easiest way to not provoke them is to sit out here," Michael would tell anyone he trained, which amounted to seventeen keepers in his almost quarter decade at the zoo.

"She'd sit in my lap back in the early days," the man often reminisced. *"Such a sweet little lady. Loved being petted."* He would show photos of the early days, when the cassowary's brown feathers resembled the stripes of a watermelon. As she grew and her adult coloring came in, Michael noticed the pleasant demeanor of the bird began to change.

One morning, as he cleaned the enclosure, Michael caught the cassowary glaring at him suspiciously. She growled lightly. Her foot came up, the claws spread apart. The middle toenail, almost four inches in length, curved out toward the keeper. Cassie did not move; there was only fifteen feet between them. *"That's no distance at all to a cassowary, mind you,"* he would remind them.

Michael lowered his head and pretended to jog toward someone each time he reached this point in the story. *"She'd be on you before your heart could thump twice."* He would trail off here as he wistfully added, *"That was the last day I stepped foot in there with her. Or least when I was alone."*

He sat down at the barrier window, where he'd fed Cassie countless times, cutting fruit into chunks large enough she could swallow them whole without choking. In the wild, she would have grabbed even bigger ones with no regard for her safety. For the most part, Cassie was always gentle at the window, but occasionally, she would swing at the barrier with her small vestigial wing, shaking the structure.

Michael finished pitting three of the plums and readied them for Cassie. The snarls and growls that often accompanied feeding time no longer gave him pause, although it was noticeably louder this night.

"You're a hungry one, aren't you, my love?" Michael said, sliding open the porthole in the barrier. A flash of pink light momentarily blinded Michael, his arm shooting up to block it.

As his vision returned, he saw the light came from Cassie herself. "What in the world?"

Cassie responded, her beak clicked four times in quick succession. Her neck shot forward through the barrier glass. One bite severed the old man's arm. He tried to scream, but the bird's mandibles gripped either side of his throat.

In one solid thrust, the bird yanked Michael Flanders into her enclosure. He was dead before he hit the ground.

CHAPTER TWO

John Chole sunk deeper into his black leather overstuffed chair. Even with a rip in the center, it was the single most comfortable place in the house, and he spent as much time there as he could. His dog, Chewie, stared at him from the couch to John's left, but John didn't notice; his mouth moving with each word of the film. He'd seen *Deadpool* something like seventy–three times, but he had to do something to pass the time. It was his first night off in over a week and yet part of him wished he could head in since he was awake anyway.

As if in answer to his thoughts, John's phone vibrated from its place on the throw blanket hanging on the armrest. The chair squeaked and groaned as he reached for the phone to check the texts.

Work: Any chance you can come in? I'll give you double time instead of time and a half.

John sat up reading the magic words. He'd been trying to save up to get his wife to Galaxy's Edge at Disneyland. "Double time? Fuck yeah."

John: Absolutely. I'll be there in 30 mins.

Work: Cool. See you soon.

John mashed the home button on his Roku remote until it went back to the main menu, without looking he tapped the power button on the other remote to turn the television off. He grabbed a dark black hoodie from the couch. Pulling it over his head, he thought, *Better leave Holly a note*. He adjusted his glasses and grabbed a pen and a piece of scrap paper. He scribbled, *Got called in to work. Love you.*

He set the note on her laptop as he shook his head, his long mop of hair needed a cut, but when did it not? Pulling on a baseball cap, he moved toward the front door. His eyes scanned the hanging calendar marked with appointments, events, school holidays, and special reminders. The roughness of the rug gave way to the cold tile of the kitchen.

He threw open the fridge, the light illuminating the otherwise dark room. Scanning through, he found only an empty soda box. "Well, crap." He removed the box, tossing it near the garbage. *I'll just stop for something, I guess.* As he closed the door, Chewie nudged his leg. John reached down to pet him and grabbed a treat for his best friend. "Here you go, buddy."

As he stepped out onto the quiet Glendale street, John looked up at the sky. The few stars that were visible through the lights and pollution made him miss living in Oregon even more. He pushed the key fob to his white Malibu and climbed in, looking up at the sky one more time, annoyed he could see more planes than stars.

The multi–lane streets were less hectic than during the day, but still not empty. John liked that at night he only had to deal with stop lights and the occasional pedestrian instead of honking cars, angry Uber drivers, delivery vans and countless emergency vehicles responding to countless accidents. He stopped at one red light with no one coming in either direction, but he wouldn't chance it. He looked over at the light pole papered with flyers for special events, ads, and gatherings that had almost definitely passed with no one taking the paper back down.

The bus shelter nearby featured a large sign advertising the exact same law firm as almost every other bus stop in the city. John made a left and pulled into the parking lot he drove into on far too many nights, inhaling the aroma of oil and grease before he even reached the drive–thru speaker.

"Welcome, would you like to try the new—"

John didn't want to try anything new, so he phased out, waiting to order what he ordered every time. "Nah, can I get six tacos please?" Tacos were John's favorite food. They were also the one thing he could order and not risk getting pickles. Who the fuck likes pickles? Who's like, *You know what I'd like to eat? A pickle*. People are ridiculous.

"Do you want any sauce with that?"

"I'm good, thanks." The lady repeated the order and rattled off the total. John pulled forward.

The small window was cracked just enough to overhear the employees chatting. The window attendant adjusted her headset as she yelled back, "Just tacos, yeah." She turned back to the window and gave him the total again. As John waited for her to run his card, he looked past her.

The drive–thru was always open, but the inside was shut down for the night. The booster chairs were stacked, so he assumed the tables had chairs on them and the booths were clean. The light from the menu boards flashed as they shuffled through some of the options. She handed John's card back. "Your food will be out in a minute."

John stared out at the small strip mall; one of hundreds in the Phoenix Metro that all featured similar stores and appeared almost identical. Each one housed a coffee shop, a fast food place or three, some no-name clothing store that no one knew how it stayed in business, and some random store that sold vintage t-shirts, comic books, and old vinyl albums.

The window opened again. The tacos rumpled the paper bag as the woman shoved them in. "Do you need any sauce?"

"No," he said again.

She looked at the tattoo on his right hand, where Jack and Sally smiled softly at one another. "Cool ink, man."

"Yeah. Uh. Thanks."

The woman's face completely morphed. Her mouth clinched shut, teeth grinding, as she pointed at the passenger side of his car, "What the fuck is that?" Her hand moved to her face, trembling.

"What?" John looked to his right. His eyes moved up the window. A small head with large glowing rose–colored eyes stared at him. The seatbelt pulled tight as John's body jolted. "Oh, holy shit."

The pink eyes slid sideways in response to the drive–thru window slamming shut. John stared at the animal, unable to register the light from its eyes reflecting in the glass, illuminating the inside of the car.

A large crown of sorts sat upon the beast's head. The casque came into better view as the bird lowered her neck. The window exploded. A large shard of glass shot into John's wrist as he screamed in pain. He reached over, pulling the car into gear. The bird's beak punctured John's forearm twice. John' pushed the pedal as the car peeled out.

The bird's head whipped off the window frame and shot out of the car. The animal's body hit the pavement. John nailed the gas, glancing up at the mirror. The left tire of the Malibu jumped the walkway on the side of the building. The car straightened out as John drove forward. He reached the exit intent on running the red, but a slow semi–truck in his way prevented it.

Behind him, a bright white flash like lightning illuminated the Jack–in–the–Box parking lot. Only it could not have been lightning, as it lasted a full three seconds. It had been too bright to look at directly, but John had done so. As his eyes tried to readjust to the darkness behind him, he saw the animal running straight at his vehicle, head down. "What the fuck?"

John looked both ways and ran the red. The back window imploded as the cassowary's body slammed the car. Talons ripped holes into the back of the Malibu. John tried to push the pedal down farther as the bird's talons punctured the roof. The claws gripped tight, holding the bird in place. The cassowary released her grasp on one side and took a step, shredding four holes in another section of the roof.

John's eyes squeezed shut as he blew through another red light, doing seventy–five. The bird's other talon released as it took another step, again puncturing the roof of the Malibu. John ground his teeth together and closed his eyes as he yanked the emergency brake.

The car slid side to side as the tires left a permanent reminder across the road. He had expected the bird to fly off the car, but it only dug its feet in more, now near the front of the vehicle.

What the fuck?

John could not tell if he'd screamed the words or only imagined doing so. He hit the gas, spinning the steering wheel to the side as hard as he could.

A loud noise shook the car. John did not know how he could identify the sound, but he knew without a doubt that the bird was pecking the top of the car. It hit again. Then again. John's arm stiffened against the steering wheel as he drove his back into the seat. His tires squealed as his brakes ground, but each was drowned out by the screech of metal sliding along the nearby wall and further glass shattering. The seat belt strap jerked against his lap as he was tossed side to side. John's head connected quickly with the driver's side window.

A sensation of time slowing filled his head as his thoughts fogged. He grew conscious of the burn of the cuts from the glass in his arm. Frustration and panic grew as his open eye locked on the blood dripping on his skin. His full body shivered. His ears rang as he coughed, the smell of gasoline and burned rubber filling the air. Blood pooled at the back of his mouth. He reached for the door handle, but it did not open. His mind said he was trying to move, but his body barely reacted. Pain throbbed through his neck as his head rolled to look left. Two glowing eyes stared right back at him.

"You gotta be kidding me."

The bird's talon shot through the window, gripping John's upper body. The middle toe of the talon dug into his back. John fell completely limp. The bird yanked back, pulling half of John Chole's body through the window. His torso splattered across McDowell Road, fifteen feet from the rest of him.

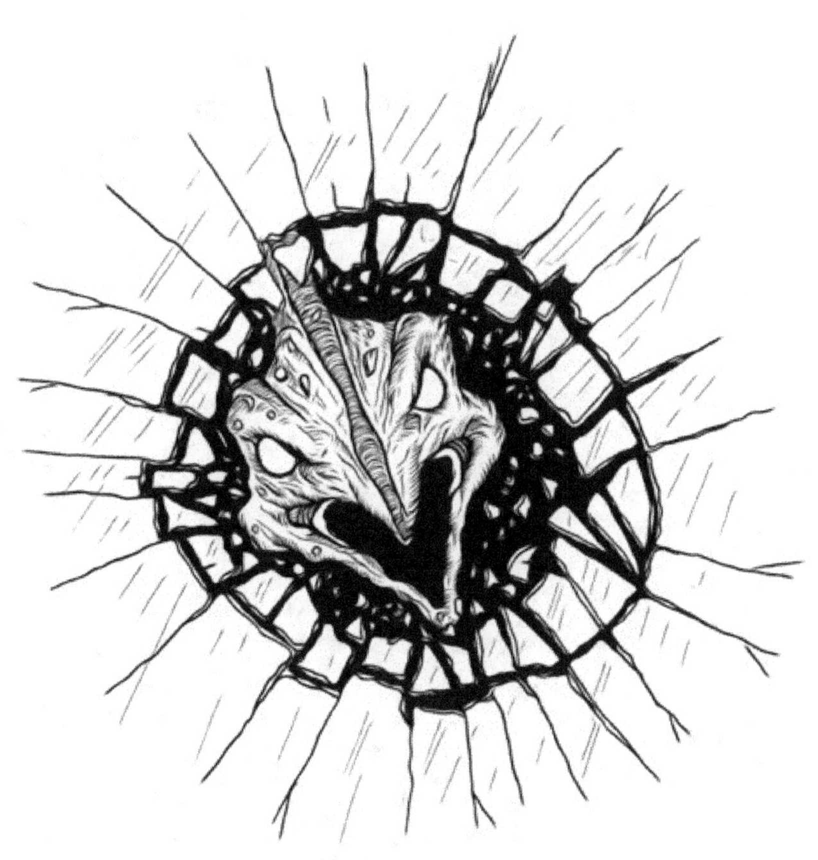

CHAPTER THREE

Cathy's brakes squealed as she pulled into her assigned spot. The jolt of the car shifting into park told her she had not come to a complete stop, but she had no time to care. The car door slammed. The beep of the car remote was followed by a quick honk.

Her heels ticked across the asphalt as she beelined for the flashing red and blue lights blocking the visitor entrance of the Toscano Wildlife Preserve. Bushes and trees framed the lot, as if the emergency vehicles had been purposely positioned with the landscaping. The ambulance at the back of the other vehicles stood with its back doors open. Police were making their way into the employee side gates.

Who let them in there? What is happening?

She inhaled deeply; the freshly mown grass and blooming desert flowers the final semblance of peace she would know for a while. She stared straight ahead as a firefighter walked toward her, sliding his thick gloves over his calloused hands.

"Ma'am, I'm going to need you to stand back."

"Well, I'm going to need you to tell me what the hell is going on." Her short red hair bobbed side to side with each enunciation. Her dark sunglasses blocked the morning light but did nothing to mask her concern at the events unfolding. She extended her hand toward the man. "Cathy Cakebread. Public Relations and Social Media Director for the Preserve." She dropped her hands. "What happened? Fire?"

Behind Cathy, three more police cars pulled into the parking lot. As the firefighter walked her through the events a police officer joined them and added further details. Cathy's eyes widened as her mouth slackened. She looked down, rubbing one eyebrow as if it would help her find words. Her blanched expression did not shift as she slowly shook her head. Her hand came up, carving a path through her freshly straightened hair. She held it back for a second before releasing.

"I don't even know what to say," her eyes not focusing on anything in particular. The tingling in her chest was more noticeable to her than her restricted breathing. A light breeze blew against her clothing, tousling her hair.

She finally managed to say, "Can I see it?"

It was an immediate judgment; neither good nor bad, right nor wrong. She just felt in the moment that more information would help her grasp what was happening.

The sidewalks cutting throughout the zoo were almost empty. The Australian habitat was closest to the front gate and just to the right. As she passed the kangaroo exhibit, the largest peeked over the gate, stoic and somber. He was just over five feet tall, but stood regally, his red pelt reflecting the sunrise.

The kangaroos were her favorite; not that she would admit it. For the most part, they were some of the most laid–back animals in the zoo, although she had once read news stories of a large Red in some village in Australia that killed a couple dozen people. She pushed the thought out of her head as it didn't help with what she knew she was about to see.

EMTs pushed past her, taking the stretcher toward the cassowary exhibit.

"I don't understand." Cathy found herself

mumbling. "The bird has always been friendly. I mean, they have a reputation, but our handlers are world class. They know what they're doing. She's never had any issues."

The police officer did not respond directly, deferring to, "It's really bad. Unlike anything I've seen. Are you sure you want to—" Cathy's expression held such authority that he stopped midquestion. His head bopped, pointing the way to the exhibit as though Cathy had not walked the grounds every day for the last seven years. Cathy walked forward, already aware that whatever she found would never be erased from her memory.

The amount of blood immediately removed any feeling that what she saw in front of her was real. It was too much blood. In a movie, it would've been a puddle under the worker's head, but Michael Flanders' face was barely recognizable.

The left half of his skull was entirely missing; a mass of gelatinous ooze squished under it, positioned perfectly like a pillow to rest his half–head on. Chunks of bloody meat were strewn through the pieces of beard remaining on the right side of his face. His lone eye hung lazily to the side. Not open in fear. Not closed. Just dangling, partially removed from the socket. His body was no better off. The left leg lay at unnatural angles, giving the impression he had two knees, and each bent a different direction. Somehow, his signature black hat still sat on his head; his sunglasses broken, some ten feet from him.

Cathy reached down and picked them up. Dried blood and hair clung to her thumb like molasses. A tear reached the corner of her eye as she set the glasses back down.

"I was just about to tell you not to touch anything." The officer mumbled.

"I need pictures."

Cathy's iPhone zoomed in and took picture after picture. She tried her best to keep Michael's body out of the photos, but she needed as much evidence as she could get as to what occurred. Focusing on the porthole in the feeding window, she zoomed in on the blood coating the broken pieces of the wall; splintered, jutting out toward her. A shiver ran up her spine as she realized Michael had been pulled through by the bird.

When she had taken more pictures than she could possibly use, Cathy walked to the double door at the back of the enclosure. Studying the door, she muttered to herself. "No damage?" Her fingers ran across the cold steel of the door. "How did the bird open the door?"

"Your security guard opened the door. That one, too," the officer said, pointing to the outer door. Cathy's head flinched back slightly.

"They were both locked?" Her stomach fluttered as she reached for answers. "Then someone had to let her out!"

Cathy walked with authority as she cleared the hallway to her office. The card reader beeped as she scanned her identification badge. The lock clicked and she pushed open the large glass door. Crossing the lush carpet in fewer steps than usual, she slid into the chair at the oversized desk flanked by two chairs that were almost never used at the same time. As she waited for the security footage, her eyes scanned the shelves on the nearby wall holding business manuals, books, and framed photography.

The chair squeaked as Cathy adjusted her leg. She noticed none of it, simply thinking about what she was about to see and what she'd already seen.

Barely blinking, Cathy Cakebread sat alone, stunned at the brutality on her screen; almost thankful it only recorded in night vision and not full color. She didn't want anyone else to see this. She wished she didn't have to see it. Michael Flanders deserved better. He hadn't just been an incredible employee. He was a good man who always cared for others; most of all, his murderer. How did this happen?

The bird rose, standing triumphantly over the fallen body of the man who had spent the better part of his life caring for her. An unnatural, radiant light coated everything near the animal's head. Is it coming from her eyes? How is that even possible? When the bird's head spun to the side and her eyes locked directly on the camera, Cathy jolted back from the computer. An anxious giggle rose as Cathy chided herself for jumping. It cut off instantly as she watched the bird jump the twelve–foot barrier like it was nothing.

"What the hell?"

Cathy rewound and pushed play several times. The cassowary, a flightless bird, glided over the enclosure wall.

Then it was gone.

CHAPTER FOUR

Jerome McClintock sat quietly perched one hundred feet in the air, a single metal bar holding him in place on The Vertigo, the tallest attraction in the zoo. The swing moved lightly with the breeze, but did not spin as it would normally when filled with riders. From his makeshift crow's nest, he could see keepers scavenging for the bird, golf carts driving down the pathways, and what looked like two of the tortoises getting in some quality time.

What he did not see, no matter where he looked, was a one–hundred–fifty pound, five–foot–tall black bird with a crown on her head.

"I got nothing," he admitted into his radio.

"Ready for dismount?" Dr. Brungardt's voice returned.

Jerome's beard reformed around his smile, as he stared out at the highway passing the zoo. "That's what she said. And no. Not even a little bit. But there's work to be done, so bring me down anyway."

His smile faded as he stared out at the front parking lot. Emergency medical services had been mostly replaced by news crews. He reached instinctively for the phone in his pocket, but the chair swung with the weight shift; each of the four chains buckling, reminding him he was still fifty feet above the earth. His text could wait a minute.

Dr. Brungardt walked toward him as Jerome landed. Jerome unfastened the buckle, waving him off.

"I'm good. I got this, Doc."

His fingers flew across his phone's keyboard as Brungardt squinted his eyes, looking around the area. "Nothing at all, huh?"

"Hang on. Let me finish sending this." He paused, read it over, and hit send. He locked eyes with the veterinarian, "Nothing. Although you might get baby tortoises soon."

"Again? Those two are worse than a couple of teenagers."

"They get more action than I do," Jerome stated, his fingers trying to adjust his collar, but missing the leather band of his necklace.

Thomas teased, "Your lady necklace is showing."

Jerome reached to adjust it. "It's not a lady necklace, asshole." He smiled. "I got this from my grandma."

"Oh. Sorry. Your little old lady necklace is showing."

The two laughed as Brungardt pointed toward the front of the zoo, adjusting his hat. "We should head up there. Cathy is looking for you."

Kaitlyn Lenhart glared at the red light as she drummed her fingers on the steering wheel. She sat a mere two blocks from the Toscano Wildlife Preserve. The cross street was completely empty. She looked left again. Then right. Her foot hit the accelerator and she made a left against the red.

Vzzzzzt. Kaitlyn grabbed the iPhone from her passenger seat without looking. Her finger slid the notification and clicked on the message.

Jerome McClintock: Hey! If you're not here yet, go to the back door. I have some bad news and I want to be the one to tell you.

Kaitlyn did not want to read any more texts. She had been preparing for this all week. Cassie, the animal she worked with more than any other, had shown signs she was not doing well. The bird had been sleeping a lot, something she never did, and eating maybe a quarter her normal diets. She was sluggish. Her pupils larger than normal, while the caramel irises had lost some of their luster. Something had been deeply wrong with Cassie for the last week and Kaitlyn knew nothing good could come from it.

She had discussed it repeatedly with Michael Flanders, Cassie's other main caretaker.

"Oh no. I hope Michael's taking the news okay," she thought, as her fingers wrapped tighter around the steering wheel. Kaitlyn tried to clear her mind of the emotions she was feeling, but another text pulled Kaitlyn immediately back into reality.

Jerome McClintock: Front is filled with news crews. I'll explain when you're here.

Kaitlyn pushed her hair out of her eye absentmindedly as she stared at the words.

News crews? Why are there news crews?

As she approached the parking lot, she saw he was not exaggerating. Every local news station was accounted for, as were some radio stations and even a couple of people who appeared to be recording out of their trunk. Whatever they were there for was a lot bigger than one dead cassowary.

Kaitlyn drove past slowly, with no intention of stopping. The next turn was almost a mile up, giving Kaitlyn plenty of space before she went around to the back of the wildlife preserve. Her hand scanned radio stations as she desperately searched for any channel talking about whatever had happened.

Dr. Thomas Brungardt stopped in the middle of hitching an animal trailer to the back of the Jeep.

"It's ironic," he said, smiling at her. "The Jeep can take on any terrain, but the trailer really can't. This is never going to work."

Before she could ask what Brungardt meant, Jerome came through the door. "Kaitlyn! There you are. I'm glad you're here. Are you okay?"

Kaitlyn shook her head no, but it moved so lightly Jerome would have missed her response if he was not looking right at her. He looked back at Dr. Brungardt. "We'll be back in a bit."

"I'll be here."

While it was not anything like she had expected, Jerome explained the full situation as they walked through the Preserve on their way to Cathy's office.

Cathy Cakebread stayed seated behind her computer, furiously typing a rough draft of the press conference announcement she did not want to make. Jerome's open palm pointed to the chair, but Kaitlyn shook her head, pacing back and forth.

Cathy locked her fingers in front of her; a personal note to herself not to type as she spoke. Her eyes stared directly at Kaitlyn. "We've watched all the video footage that we can. A lot of the security cameras have been having issues the last few days. But suffice it to say, we don't believe she's here. Jerome is going out to look for the cassowary. We've wasted a lot of time searching the zoo and we need to get outside these walls and find her before someone else does. He's requested that you go with him."

Kaitlyn's brows lowered as her eyes narrowed.

"Me? I'm not security. I don't know that I'd be..."

Jerome cut her off. "I've got the security part taken care of. I want someone who can make the bird feel comfortable and you're now the person who knows Cassie the best." He forced a smile to make her feel more at ease, but it did the opposite. "You're the one who loves her the most. I think she'll respond to you."

Cathy produced a smile, her hair waving lightly in her face as she spoke. "Dr. Brungardt will be there with you as well, so you'll be safe." The chair squeaked lightly as Cathy returned to typing. "He'll be there in case Cassie is injured and needs any immediate care."

Kaitlyn smiled wearily. "We'll bring her home."

Cathy looked up, smiling gently. "I hope so." Her smile faded as she turned to Jerome. "I just got the okay. Let's get your weapons."

The trio walked into the General Curator's office, which resembled a larger version of Cathy's office with two storage cabinets at the far end of the room. Cathy unlocked both and turned to Jerome. "What do you think you'll need?"

Jerome took a quick mental inventory of the cabinet, analyzing the firearms, tranquilizer guns, pepper spray, catch poles, net guns, tarpaulins, and first aid kits used by the Emergency Response Team. He handed Kaitlyn two Dan–Inject Dart Guns as he grabbed another. He additionally grabbed a 30.06.

Cathy locked the cabinets as Jerome signed everything out. No one in the room spoke for almost thirty seconds. Finally, Kaitlyn managed, "We'll be back as soon as we can. Keep us up to date with any changes. Do you have my phone number?"

"Who's ready to catch a dinosaur?" Thomas Brungardt beamed from under his hat.

"This isn't Jurassic Park, man," Jerome said.

"Really?" Dr. Brungardt feigned disappointment as he lowered his head. "But I spared no expense getting my degree so I could have this job." He threw his bag of tools into the back of the Jeep. "You know, speaking from an evolutionary point of view, cassowaries are much more closely related to velociraptors than they are other birds. Not to mention their breast plates and sternums are not developed enough to fly or even really designed to do so."

Jerome ignored him, concentrating fully on Kaitlyn. Kaitlyn's shoulders slouched as she positioned herself in the passenger seat. Her hand quickly swiped at her left cheek. Jerome tried to remain cheery,

"Hey. We're gonna find her. It will be okay." He pulled his seatbelt across his chest and turned the key as the buckle clicked.

Kaitlyn's chest was tight as she exhaled the breath she had been holding for a few seconds. Her vision blurred quickly before returning to normal. She took another deep breath and smiled. "I know. I'm not worried. Let's do it."

Hunter Womack stood fifteen feet from John Chole's car— the exact distance Glendale PD stated he had to stay back. The wind repositioned his blond hair, but he pushed it out of his eyes with his left hand. His lips moved as he read the words on his phone. He glanced up, just long enough to watch Liz Hansen remove a microphone and a boom stand from the Channel 3 Eyewitness News Van.

Liz walked toward him, a Canon XA11 in one hand and the boom in the other. "Cramming for a big test, Hunter?"

"Just learning about the bird that did this." He looked out at John Chole's car. "These things run thirty–five miles per hour. Jump six feet in the air. And look at these legs."

Liz turned the phone so she could see it better. The cassowary's legs looked straight out of a sci–fi movie, with long, hard, tree trunks layered in age-old scales descending into forked tridents, each toe pointing a different direction, a razor sharp nail on each foot, the middle toe's nail long and polished like a knife blade awaiting prey.

"Holy shit. You weren't kidding about the dinosaur comparison," Liz muttered.

"Right?"

Liz opened the bottom of the boom stand, the feet shooting in three sixty–degree angles from one another. Hunter found his mark as Liz started the camera.

"How's this?"

"Two steps left," came her reply as she framed the shot. "There. That looks great. You ready?"

"Ready."

"Five. Four. Three." She held up two fingers. Then one.

Hunter faced the camera, his face more serious than ever. "An escaped animal. A dead zookeeper and this…" His palm extended toward the remains of John Chole's car. "I'm Hunter Womack and *THIS* is Channel 3 Eyewitness News."

CHAPTER FIVE

The trio drove in near silence. Occasionally Dr. Brungardt leaned forward to make a remark about the area, but for the most part, he and Kaitlyn concentrated on the environment around them.

"You know, cassowaries are almost impossible to find. Even when we do know exactly where they are." Brungardt said aloud; although even he did not know if it was directed at everyone or mostly himself. Staring at her phone, Kaitlyn tried to make out the area in the screenshot Cathy forwarded.

"I still don't know why she couldn't just give us the actual tracker so we could do this better."

"Security," Jerome muttered with a small huff.

"It's gotta be right in this area. Those two trees are the only ones that could be the ones on the map she sent," Kaitlyn said, again scanning the trees and rocks around them.

Brungardt pushed his glasses up his nose as he added, "Some wildlife researchers report staring directly at a cassowary in the trees in New Guinea and they still can't see it. You'd think something that big would be obvious. The head is bright blue, for Christ's sake. But nah. They just blend in wherever they are."

"She might not even still be here," Jerome said. "I think we should go back to the zoo and demand the tracker."

"Kind of like how my words apparently just disappear even when you're both sitting right here." Brungardt smiled. Jerome rolled his eyes. It was all the response his friend needed. "What about your uncle? He's a tracker."

"Wrong type of tracker."

"No way, man! If he can stalk down a baby javelina he hears crying two blocks away, I'm pretty sure he can help us with this." Brungardt shrugged. "Plus, it would be nice if we had a little more muscle to put this bird in the trailer if we do succeed."

"When we succeed," Kaitlyn added.

Jerome shook his head. "And we don't need to go see my uncle. We'll be fine without him. He probably wouldn't help us anyway," Jerome sputtered. "He's busy with Grandma's estate stuff."

Kaitlyn smiled. "Who else do you know who can catch this bird?"

"No one. Although truthfully, I don't know if anyone can catch it."

Kaitlyn stared at him. Jerome stared back, his foot coming off the gas as he did so. The two held eye contact until he looked at her lips. The way they shined made him want to kiss her worse than ever. Kaitlyn slowly said, "Someone is going to find this bird. I need it to be you and me."

Jerome slowly repeated the part he cared about. "You and me."

Brungardt sat with his palms out. "What am I? Chopped liver?"

Jerome shrugged. "You know what Uncle Kevin does have? A shitload of firepower. And we might need something better than what they gave us."

Kaitlyn stiffened. "Our orders are to bring the cassowary back alive."

Jerome grinned. "Yes and having more real guns along might help us scare the bird enough to run where we need her to in order to use the tranquilizers."

Brungardt made eye contact with Kaitlyn, his usual smirk nowhere to be found. "We're going to do our best, you know? But often times these things just don't work out. We have to be prepared for anything. It's not out of line to think we'll probably need firepower for a different reason. And a bird that size? We need more than a simple shotgun."

Jerome added, "He's really good with animals in the wild. It's a different world than we're used to."

Kaitlyn sat in silence, her head and shoulder pushed into the passenger side window as if she couldn't get far enough away from the reality around her. She released a long sigh. "How far away is he?"

"He lives less than ten minutes from here."

She shook her head. "Okay. Let's at least go visit Kevin and see if he has any ideas, but we can't be there too long. We need to be the ones to find her."

Jerome handed Kaitlyn his phone. "Can you please send him a text. See if we can come over." Kaitlyn stared at the lock screen.

"I don't know your password."

"It's your birthday." Jerome smiled.

Kaitlyn flinched back, her lip curling as her gaping mouth pulled an audible intake of breath. Jerome's laughter broke the moment.

"I'm fucking kidding. Good lord." His finger quickly drew a square root sign and the phone opened. Kaitlyn's phone buzzed.

"Hang on! It's Cathy." Kaitlyn's finger slid to open her own phone. The picture loaded, showing the updated location of the animal. "Cassie's farther north. She's just on this side of Cactus and Bullard."

Jerome floored the gas pedal trying to outrun his friend, but each time he looked in the rearview, Thomas was still there.

Thomas had always been there for him. The two met the first day Jerome started working at the Toscano Wildlife Preserve. Dr. Thomas Brungardt introduced himself immediately and the two hit it off discussing the music Brungardt blasted through his earbuds. Before long, they found themselves at an Irish pub next to the hockey stadium.

The combined odor of deep-fried foods, yeasty beers, and stale whiskey breath greeted them at the door. As in most pubs, the dimly lit interior was aided through the flashing light emanating from the flat screens spaced around the room. Men sat at the long wooden bar staring at the local craft beer taps and the selection of international brews, questioning which to try next while ignoring the ones already in their hands.

Todd waved the two men in from behind the bar as he plucked two cherries out of the garnish bin and dropped them in a fellow's Coke. A waitress dressed in cutoffs bent over the closest booth; one hand holding the remains of a recently eaten dinner, the other expertly swiping the table to prepare it for the next patron. Pens and a notepad dangled from her mini pouch apron, threatening to fall to the floor. She stood up, saving them just in time as she blew a stray strand of hair out of her face.

"Good afternoon. Grab a chair wherever you like. Booth, bar, whatever."

Over the course of the next three hours, the two men found they shared a love of the same movies, many of the same sports teams, and so many of the same beers that they had to get to know each other all over again the following week. It was Thomas that first talked to the waitress for Jerome and it was Thomas who helped get Jerome his first date with her. It was Thomas who helped his friend back up when that same waitress left him for a drummer who couldn't sing. It was Thomas who helped him find the next girl.

Thomas wouldn't help him with Kaitlyn.

"It's too soon. She just broke up with that one guy." He would say. "And you can't date someone you work with. It's messy. They know too much. You have to see them again. Worst of all, they talk to one another. You don't want dates talking to one another. You only have so many moves in your repertoire. You want them sending out spoilers?"

Thomas had wrapped his hand on his friend's shoulder. "You're not ready for a Kaitlyn. She's too independent. Too focused on her own goals."

Jerome knew then he was on his own. And while he understood Kaitlyn needed time to heal, he also knew that when a girl looked like her, there was only a small window of time before the next boyfriend arrived.

"There!" Kaitlyn's voice broke Jerome's thoughts. Her outstretched arm ended with her pointer finger locked on the animal. "She's right there."

"Holy shit. There she is!" Jerome said as he pulled the vehicle to the side of the road. The empty trailer wobbled as it hit the shoulder.

Brungardt reached forward, handing one of the dart guns to Jerome. Kaitlyn threw the door of the Jeep open, racing toward the bird.

"She's a fast one! You're going to need one of these to just to keep up with her," Brungardt said.

Jerome smiled. "The thought has occurred to me."

"I meant the bird." Brungardt's teeth crunched together at his friend's response, but he thought better of adding to it.

The two men pushed through the tall grass and wildflowers, following their friend. Kaitlyn had locked eyes on the bird and not let up. She followed the animal into an area overgrown with bushes and trees, used as a wall on the edge of a golf course. But all of her tracking skills weren't enough as the animal camouflaged into the brush and she disappeared completely.

Kaitlyn dug through pieces of the brush, as quietly as she could. If the bird was in there, she couldn't risk being pecked or even scaring her. Kaitlyn found nothing. She threw her arms out.

"What the hell?" The wind rustled the leaves as birds called and squirrels chattered in the distance. Kaitlyn thought she could hear the cassowary in the distance rooting around the underbrush, but there was no way to know if it was just her imagination.

Jerome arrived, grabbing her forearm with his hand and pulling Kaitlyn back. He pushed forward, the dart gun close to his chest, as he assumed command of the mission. He held a finger to his lips to keep the others quiet before pointing ahead and to the left. The trio moved in relative silence until Brungardt's shoe accidentally connected with a pinecone. It skidded across the dry dirt, before connecting with the base of another tree. Jerome pressed his palm into Brungardt's chest before again holding a single finger to his own mouth. The doctor rolled his eyes as they continued.

Pushing farther through the wooded area, Kaitlyn found an opening. The two men followed her through it, finding themselves in the middle of a large section of greenery and well–tended landscaping. The dart gun lowered from his chest as Jerome looked all around.

The only bird in sight was a duck sitting in the shade of a tree near the fourteenth hole.

A deep sigh emanated from his lungs. "Hold this, please." He pulled out his phone.

Kaitlyn took the dart gun. Her head turned sideways. "Who are you calling?"

Jerome didn't look up as his fingers danced across the keypad. "I'm texting Uncle Kevin. We clearly need help."

CHAPTER SIX

"You haven't beaten me in over fifteen years!" Tim smirked as he pulled a knitted head cover from a set of clubs and removed a 3–wood. His blindingly yellow and blue tartan sweater vest was a look only he could pull off.

Adam Goldman rolled his eyes behind his old friend's back as he traded his street shoes for golf shoes. "We haven't played in fifteen years. Ha Ha. Very funny."

"Whatever, Mr. Rogers."

Adam stared at the label of the bottle Tim had presented to him earlier that morning. "You know this shit is a million times better than what I'm used to, right?"

"I bought it. Of course I know that. Four Roses. Limited Edition. Small batch. The liquor is old enough to drink itself legally." Tim turned to watch his friend. "You gonna open it or what? But take it slow. I need you to get through all eighteen holes or I'll have to drive the cart all the way back to wherever you pass out. We both know I'm too old to carry your fat ass."

Adam shook his head. "Man, I missed your dumb face."

Tim nodded, wiggling his back side. "It's been far too long." His smile disappeared. "Just happy I could come visit, man." He pushed the ball and the tee into the soft ground. His hand repeatedly flexed as he fit his fingers firmly around the grip of the club. Tim widened his stance, mentally practicing the shot.

His eyebrows raised. "Sorry, you're going to have to spend your whole day following shots like this one." The club made a light woosh as he took a practice swing. Tim pulled himself into position and swung for real. The tick of the ball echoed as they watched the little white orb coast through the air down the fairway.

Adam removed the two glasses Tim included with the bourbon. He poured three fingers into each and held one out to Tim.

Tim stared at him. "Yeah, I guess I better have some of this before you down it all." Eyes closed, he inhaled the scent before enjoying a sip.

Adam lined up his shot and swung. His right hand shaded his eyes as he watched his ball try to catch up with Tim's.

The two men took their respective seats in the golf cart, their bags bouncing along the bumpy terrain. Tim smiled, "So, this is how you spend every Saturday morning?"

"I try to. Been doing it for a couple years now. I've become such a regular they offered to let me come in even earlier. Didn't add much to my bill and I never have to wait for someone to play through." Tim listened to the rattle of the clubs hitting one another as he sipped his bourbon. Adam inhaled the combination of gas and fresh cut grass. He stopped the cart just off the fairway. "Top you off?"

Tim shook his head. "Not yet, thank you. I know you can't beat me fairly, but it's too early to get me too drunk."

The two men played through the first five holes. Hole six was a simple par three. Tim lined up his shot. "Your experience on this course has given you a small lead, but now's my time to shine. I just need a birdie or a hole in one."

"And I just need to win the lottery."

The ball flew to the green, bounced twice and rolled right past the hole before coming to a stop. Tim adjusted his ball cap. "Let's see you do better than that."

Adam smiled. "Sure enough. I'll just put it right in the hole."

Tim shook his head, enjoying his fifth and sixth fingers of bourbon. He didn't normally drink much, but this trip was an exception and he planned to relish as much of it as he possibly could.

Adam lined up the swing and took his shot. His hand cupped his eyes as he watched the white ball rise into the air and come back down. It sliced hard toward the trees to the left of the green. "Hey Tim... what do you make of that?" Adam watched as a six-foot–tall black bird stood pecking navel oranges off one of the trees.

Tim's head raised slowly. "What?" His eyes grew. "Holy shit." His hand gripped his friend's shoulder. "What the hell is that?"

"Clear as day. That's your birdie you wanted."

The Lovecraftian turkey seemed to pay no attention to them as its large reptilian feet dug at the rough with each step, seemingly seeking a shady place to rest.

Adam went to fill his empty glass. "Not much else we can do while we wait, I suppose. I'm not getting my ball while that thing is standing there." The cassowary's bright blue neck craned; her head tilting in a new direction with every sound around her.

Tim's brow squished together. "What's going on with his eyes?" An overpowering light radiated from where the animal's eyes should have been. Before Adam could answer, the bird reached the green.

"We're trying to play through," he shouted. "Get your own tee time." The animal paid no attention to him, as it sank into the turf. Adam stared at its feet. Each foot split into three toes pointing in different directions. The middle toe had a toenail almost five inches long, resembling a railroad spike. That nail pushed into the turf of the green as the large animal took two more steps. It stood, perfectly still, facing away from the two men: its foot mere centimeters from Tim's ball.

Adam pointed. "You think he's going to knock your ball in for you?"

"Well, I suppose if he does, I get a hole in one as well." Tim drew a long sip from his glass and then licked his lips. "I didn't hit it again, so it doesn't add to the stroke count."

"Still trying to justify your cheating after all these years, huh?"

Both men gasped as the cassowary's neck shot downward and the bird swallowed the ball whole.

"Son of a bitch! That's my ball!" Tim yelled.

Adam's laughter bellowed. "Gotta play it as it lies."

The sand wedge slid into Tim's hand. He turned, anger flaring in his cheeks. "Mother fucker gonna die." Adam's hands wrapped around the golf club.

"Are you insane? That bird will destroy you. You can't just beat a bird with a golf club."

Light streamed from the eyes of the bird. Her head lowered, casque pointed like the tip of a jousting lance. She held eye contact, locked on her opponent, running straight and true. Tim had no time to find a lance of his own and the sand wedge proved to be no help. The bird's casque connected with Tim's chest before either man processed the animal's movements. Tim landed, folding in on himself. His coughs echoed through the air. Blood sprayed onto his hand as his chest contorted with each heave of his lungs.

Tim reached into his pocket, removing his cell

phone. The screen had cracked from the impact of the fall. Bloody fingerprints appeared on his phone as he pushed each icon to call for help. Each push was harder and lasted longer than necessary, but he needed to make sure it went through.

"*Nine–one–one. What's the emergency?*"

Tim's skin shone with sweat as he coughed. "Attacked at the golf course."

"*Which course, sir?*" It was a reasonable question in a city with over two–hundred courses. "Fuckin' somfin."

"*Excuse me? I couldn't make that out.*"

"FALL CAN SOME DING."

"*Falcon something? Oh! Oh! Falcon. Do you know if you're North or South of Luke Air Force Base?*"

"Norfffff. By da doo."

"*By the zoo. Got it. Do you know what hole you're on? Can you tell me where on that hole on the course?*" Tim whimpered as Adam screamed in the background. The voice on the other end said, "*I have officers and an ambulance coming to you as fast as they can. Please stay calm. Tell me your name. Keep talking to me. Stay with me, okay? Try to tell me exactly what happened.*"

Adam gripped the golf club and backed away from the bird, which had come to a stop. They stared at one another. The cassowary taking one step closer for approximately every seven breaths Adam took; and those breaths came fast. The cassowary stood directly between Adam and the golf cart, his small pocketknife more than useless in the side pocket of his bag and on the cart.

And what were you going to do with it anyway? Give him a little stabby stab? Try to prop his mouth open so he doesn't swallow you whole?

Adam took a step back as the animal drew closer. He pulled the club back like a baseball bat. The bird lunged. Adam swung.

CRACK!

The club connected. The bird's head spun completely around as her neck bones shattered. The cassowary dropped to the ground all at once. Grayish bone protruded through the blue visage. The bright waddle lay to one side, losing color. The light pink in the eyes had been extinguished.

"Holy fucking shit." Adam dropped the club, staring at his hands covered in blood from the spray as the club connected. His voice shook. "Holy. Fucking. Shit." Adam took a step back, eyes bulging, blinking rapidly as he tried to process what had happened. Cold set over his core. His fingers numbed as he stared at the dead bird.

Tim's vision blurred. Everything around him spun. Blood ran into his mouth from his nose. His skin tingled. He started to call out, "The ambulance is on its—"

A blinding pink hue overpowered the daylight around them. It was everywhere at once, shooting out of the cassowary in every direction imaginable. The light stopped streaming, midair, reversed course and immediately returned to the cassowary's body. Tim's mouth fell open, the upper lip curling back into a grimace. He wanted to look away, but it proved impossible. His eyebrows folded inward; his nose crinkling as he swallowed rapidly.

The cassowary rose to her feet. The beak split open. A scream escaped the bird, as its eyes glowed brighter than before. Adam turned to run. On the seventeenth step, the beak ripped through his back, severing his spine. Adam didn't even have time to fall to the ground. His lifeless body skewered on the neck of the cassowary. The bird turned back, strutting triumphantly toward Tim. He had set his phone down at some point, but they were still on the line. It did not matter. *No one can save me.*

The bird flung its head to the side. Adam's lifeless body rose and fell, collapsing on the rough. Tim backed up, branches scraping against his shirt, but he was still unable to stand. As the bird towered over him, Tim thought, *He grew? How is he so much bigger than before?*

The beak shot forward, gripping the edges of Tim's right eye. With one quick motion, the bird tore the eye directly from the socket. The optic nerve severed instantly, hanging loosely, waving back and forth as the bird sucked it into her mouth. The cassowary stepped forward, standing directly on top of Tim. Seven ribs snapped in quick succession under the weight of the animal. The claws tore into his skin as Tim's one eye filled with tears.

CHAPTER SEVEN

"Why do they even have wings?" Jerome shrugged.

"Same as ostriches. They can't use them for flying either," Dr. Brungardt responded. "Still they use them in mating ritual dances and sometimes to redirect air to fan themselves. Things like that."

"Sounds useless."

"You're just jealous your own dance moves can't do the same." Brungardt smiled, sliding in his seat. "Cassowary wing feathers are basically like porcupine quills. They couldn't fly if they wanted to. But the weirdest part is each wing has a huge, hooked claw. And no one who studies them knows what the hell it's for."

Jerome's phone buzzed. He glanced at Kaitlyn in the passenger seat. "Can you grab that?

Kaitlyn read the message to herself, her lips moving with each syllable. She looked up, "Kevin says he's home going through your grandmother's stuff for the estate sale."

Dr. Brungardt leaned forward from the backseat. "I'm so excited. I haven't seen your crazy Uncle Kevin in probably a year." He pulled back a little. "Well, I guess at your grandmother's funeral, but not other than that."

Jerome locked eyes with his friend in the rear view." First, that wasn't even two months ago. It hasn't been that long. And he didn't do anything that weird other than the thing with the skateboard."

He shrugged. "He's not crazy. He just does things his own way."

Kaitlyn's lip raised in a smile. "Is this the uncle who once shot a car just because it was abandoned in the desert?"

Jerome smiled. "Yeah, but he didn't know that homeless dude was sleeping in there."

"It's happened to all of us." Her smile faded. "Do you think he's really going to help us catch Cassie?"

Brungardt smiled, lacing his fingers behind his head as he leaned back. "Knowing Kevin, he'll probably chase Cassie down, saddle her, and ride off into the sunset!"

Jerome nodded. "That sounds about right.

"There it is." Jerome pointed at the small single–family home on the right that looked exactly like every other single–family home on the street. While there were minor differences between the houses, the biggest difference seemed to be which HOA approved color scheme each owner selected.

As the Jeep and trailer came to a stop, Brungardt leaned forward again. "This was your grandmother's house?"

Jerome nodded. "Yeah. Uncle Kevin's been basically living there since he's in charge of the estate sale and getting everything ready and stuff."

The smile that spread across Thomas' face was almost unnatural. "I can't wait to see that fucking cat." Jerome turned the ignition off, looking back.

"Ah, shit, man. I thought I told you. Majerle passed away."

Brungardt held a hand up. "Bullshit! That cat has outlived like seven generations of your family or some shit."

Jerome laughed. "Good god. No. He was old, but not immortal. It just felt that way."

56

Brungardt opened his door, "First cat I've ever seen clearly using eight of his lives. I literally have a degree in this. There's no way that cat should have survived getting run over by that second car."

Kaitlyn reached for the door handle, but Jerome stopped her. "Hey. Before we go in, you should know he has his snakes in there."

"And?"

"I didn't want them to scare you."

Kaitlyn smirked. "You know I work in a zoo, right?"

"I'm still scared of stuff." Jerome shrugged.

Kaitlyn put a hand on his shoulder and whispered, "Don't worry. I'll protect you."

She got out of the Jeep, stretching her arms high above her head. Jerome watched as Kaitlyn's shirt rode up slightly in the back.

Thomas was suddenly next to his ear. "So we going in or are you going to just sit her and stare at her all day?"

Jerome reached for the door handle. "Shut the fuck up."

As Jerome walked around the front of the Jeep, he neared Kaitlyn. "Uncle Kevin is awesome. You're going to love him. One time when I was here, he swung a sidewinder over his head.

"Sidewinder?" Kaitlyn gasped.

Jerome shrugged it off. "It's fine. It was a baby. But in all seriousness, he's been living here for a couple weeks. His snakes are definitely in there. Don't worry. They're in their aquariums. They're not just walking around."

"Yeah, then they'd be lizards." Brungardt added with no hint of humor.

Kaitlyn's lips pressed together to suppress a smile. "Still not afraid of snakes, but okay."

Jerome crossed the weedy landscaping, took

two quick steps and bounced across the porch. One foot was still raised behind him as his fist tapped a beat to let Kevin know they had arrived. A dog barked from inside to say the message had been received.

Kaitlyn kicked at the loose gravel underfoot, looking around the neighborhood as she followed Thomas. The homes lay very close to one another. Narrow dirt or gravel alleys with ruts ran on the side of some of them. Others featured stepping stones overgrown with grass. She counted four sun–worn patio shades, six toolsheds, seven toys randomly strewn in yards, two flamingos and a lot of rusted lawn furniture. Almost everyone had flags in their yards or on their trucks.

The screen door screeched open as Kevin stepped out. "Hey, Kid. How's it going?"

"Hey, Uncle Kev. This is Kaitlyn."

Kaitlyn held out a hand. "Good to meet you."

Kevin's arms opened, as he held his beer in one hand. "Fuck handshakes. We're huggers here."

Kaitlyn shrugged and gave in, hugging him; her eyes locked on the dead petunias in the hanging planters. Kevin's mouth was near her neck as he said, "Especially with good looking women like you."

Thomas opened his arms for a hug. "Great to see you again, Kevin!"

Kevin stared at him. "I'm not hugging you." Brungardt lowered his arms as Kevin started laughing. He threw his arms around the doctor. "I'm kidding, asshole! How have you been?"

The dog's chain dragged on the wooden floor as he paced. Kevin pointed in, "Get your asses in here or the damn dog's gonna go insane."

Kaitlyn joined Jerome and his uncle at the kitchen table. It was obvious where Kevin normally ate, as that side of the table was clean, while the other was piled high with papers, boxes, and random knick knacks. The pictures on the wall were all black and white and each featured Majerle, Jerome's grandmother's cat.

No matter how many times Kaitlyn saw pictures of Majerle, she was always amazed by his sheer mass. The cat was reportedly around forty–two pounds right before his death; in pictures he appeared even larger.

"That's Majerle," Kevin said, rubbing the angel tattoo on his right forearm. "He most recently died last month. Damn thing just got bigger every couple of years."

"Most recently died?" Kaitlyn repeated.

Jerome laughed. "Cats don't die multiple times. He'd survived worse though. Hit by two cars, electrocuted—"

"Oh! That time I accidentally shot him!" Kevin's chin tucked against his neck as he laughed. "That was fucking funny."

"I told you that thing used multiple lives," Brungardt called, as he looked at the snakes in the tanks on the other side of the room.

The other two nodded along. "Something like that," Kevin muttered. He turned back toward Brungardt. "Sorry I don't have any awesome cobras and shit like you're used to at the zoo. Although I'm willing to take a cobra off your hands if you ever feel like making one disappear."

Jerome slapped Kevin on the shoulder. "Knock it off."

"So, what do you guys want? You two need the spare bedroom or something?"

A flush crept along Jerome's cheeks. His chin dipped and his feet shuffled. "What? No. Nothing like that." He disappeared down the hall into the back bedrooms as Kaitlyn laid out everything they knew about the cassowary escaping.

Kevin interrupted. "That giant bird that escaped? The one that's murdering people? Looks like an ostrich fucked a peacock?"

Kaitlyn certainly never thought of it that way before, but he did have a point. She swallowed hard. "It killed one person. A coworker. Yes, but—"

Kevin cut her off. "Oh no. It's all over the Channel 3 Eyewitness News. It fucked up a car and sliced a dude in half. They know because of the footprints on what's left of the roof. Here. Let me find it on Twitter. They'll have pics." He scrolled as he continued. "Oh shit! Looks like it got a couple dudes on a golf course too!"

"Golf course?" Kaitlyn jumped up. Jerome instinctively grabbed her, but Kaitlyn pushed him away. "So, she was still there. And now she killed someone because we didn't stop her."

"Well, I doubt there's shit you could do about that," Kevin said, pushing back in his chair until it rested on the wall. His snapback shaded his eyes from the dining room overhead light, but his eyebrow raised just the same. "You looking to kill it or catch it?"

"Catch it," Kaitlyn answered.

"You best find it before the cops do then." Kevin mulled it over a bit. "I mean, I guess if you had access to tranquilizers *and* you could keep up with its speed..." He trailed off and then added, "How fast is it?"

"Around thirty miles–per–hour," Brungardt answered, as he knelt in front of a python.

Kaitlyn scrolled through her own social media feed. "Can you help us? We could really use someone who is a good tracker."

"J. Michael's a better shot than almost anyone," he said, pointing at his nephew as Jerome returned, holding three high–powered rifles. Jerome rolled his eyes. He hated being called J. Michael and was glad only his uncle still called him that. "Tranqs or bullets, he's your guy."

"We need more than one person. He can't handle it alone," Kaitlyn volunteered, glaring at the firearms.

Kevin stared at Kaitlyn. "You don't know how to use a gun?"

Kaitlyn smiled. "Cassie is like family to me. I don't trust myself to take that shot."

Kevin leaned back. "Shit. J. Michael over there is family. I'd shoot him just to have a good story to tell people."

Jerome's head bobbed back and forth. "This bird is... different." He stared at the table while absentmindedly touching the chain around his neck.

Brungardt stood. "He needs a good shooter." He shrugged, palms out. "I'm a lover, not a fighter."

Kevin spun around. "Don't you have to dart animals for your job?"

Brungardt adjusted his hat. "Not really. That's what I have him for." He pointed at Jerome.

Kevin sat silently for a second, scrolling through his Facebook feed until the sounds of children playing on a nearby lawn drew his attention. "Well, it looks like J. Michael's got the firepower to stop her. I'd like to do more, but I can't go out and do this. And you shouldn't be either. You know they're talking about sending the military after it? The boys at Luke Airforce Base are probably counting down the seconds hoping to shoot something with permission for once. With all the crime in the West Valley you'd think someone would just shoot it themselves."

"That's what I'm afraid of," Kaitlyn said, moving the hair out of her eyes. As she did, she saw a dark shadow slither across the kitchen floor not five feet from her.

Jerome watched her eyes grow big and took his

shot to save her.

Kaitlyn's palm slammed into Jerome's chest, pushing him backward. In one motion, she bent, scooping up the Kingsnake in her hand. She held the animal near her face to get a better look at him in the kitchen light. "Look at you, little guy."

Kevin smiled, reaching out for the snake. "That's KJ. I've been looking everywhere for him. He got out of the terrarium a couple days ago. He's a regular Houdini." Kevin scooped the snake up in his hands, planting a little kiss on the reptile's back. "Hey, bubba. I'll bet you're hungry. Let me thaw you a mouse."

He looked back at Kaitlyn. "If there's one thing Kingsnakes are good at it's escaping. You give them the smallest exit and they'll find it and exploit it. They're still a hell of a lot easier to deal with than that cat mom used to have. That sucker was mean. I still have bite marks on my wrist."

"We need to be going, Mr. Lewis. But thank you for the supplies."

"Please, Kaitlyn, call me Crank. Everyone else does."

She stared at him.

His goatee split into a smile. "Or Kevin. Whatever works for you. Mr. Lewis is fine I guess."

Jerome stood, leading the others back to the front door. Dr. Brungardt threw his arms around Kevin. "It was so good to see you, Uncle Kevin."

"Get the hell off me." He clapped Brungardt on the back. "Hey, when are you gonna update your YouTube?"

Thomas laughed, "The kids' channel? You're still watching that? I'll try to get another video up this week. Just for you. What animal should I do?"

"Well, the cobra, of course."

Thomas threw out his hands. "Fine. I'll do the cobra. Just for you."

"Now you get a hug." Kevin pulled him in. Brungardt held on a little too long, so Kevin just pushed him off. "Slow down, doc, or I'll have to charge you two more videos. And don't touch my butt."

He turned, arms out, toward Kaitlyn, who hugged him solely out of obligation. As she did so, her eyes locked on another photo on the wall.

The photo showed Kevin at his seventh birthday party. The cigarettes in the ash tray next to the cake and the basketball shorts and tank top Kevin wore each screamed the photo was taken in the late eighties. Little Kevin was bent forward, blowing out the candle, the same smirk on his face that he got now when hugging attractive women, apparently. His mother sat nearby, a Budweiser in one hand and the lighter in the other. Her head thrown back; her laughter caught in the picture forever. Kaitlyn snapped two pictures of the photo and then zoomed in, focusing only on the old woman's lap, where Majerle sat purring some thirty years before.

CHAPTER EIGHT

Fifteen flags fluttered at the top of the scoreboard. Each represented one of the Major League Baseball teams that called the Cactus League home for the first few months of each year. Alayna Amaro counted those flags each morning as she walked through the stadium; a quick reminder that while she worked directly for one of those teams, at the end of the day, her job as the Vice President of Marketing and Development was to ensure fans of every team were entertained.

Sergio Abellan waved to her from his sidewinder rotary mower as he turned. Alayna waved back, always amazed at the work that went into the art of striping the grass on the field. The line coming toward her was dark green. The one Sergio mowed as he moved away from her was lighter, the rollers laying the grass ever so slightly in a different direction; the same way the nap of velour changes with a hand stroke.

The field she had worked at in Pennsylvania had a diamond shape cut in, but the grounds crew at Surprise Stadium went the extra mile, cutting different shapes into the green turf each week. Sergio's mower updated the sun they had shaped a few days before. Striping mainly benefited those sitting in the stands, as it's hard to see up close, but Alayna looked forward to seeing what Sergio and his crew would create each week.

As she walked the concourse, Alayna stopped at the tables near the concession stands or outside the spring training shops, scribbling in her notepad before continuing. The batting cages stood empty; the crack of the bat would fill the air on a normal day as people gathered round to see their favorite players take practice swings. But this was no normal day.

Her eyes scanned every sign and banner she had read hundreds of times before. "UPPER DECK — BEER FLIGHTS, GREAT COCKTAILS, AND A GREAT VIEW OF THE GAME! ALL FANS WELCOME." The rest offered hot dogs, burgers, chicken, and Carolina pulled pork. It was not even 8AM, but a burger and beer sounded delicious.

Setting down her phone for a second, Alayna looked out at the field just as the cassowary appeared. The dark body seemed to hover above the grass. The blue leather of the skin was not visible from where Alayna stood, but she could see the head bobble in response to sounds throughout the stadium. The large raptor–like feet of the cassowary came into view as Alayna realized she was not looking at a small bird up close, but a very large bird far away.

"What the fuck is an ostrich doing here?" Alayna's nails clicked her iPhone screen texting security.

Alayna: Need help. Pronto. Ostrich on the field. No really.

She took the first narrow aisle of cement stairs from the concourse to the field, her right hand holding her cell phone to record the incident; her left holding the metal rail slowly warming in the Arizona sun. She felt each step in her lower back as she made her way down, never taking the camera off the cassowary.

Climbing over the wall separating the crowd from the field, Alayna managed to land on both feet. The sharp, fresh scent of newly mown grass drifted on the lazy breeze, reminding Alayna she wasn't alone.

Sergio Abellan slowed the Toro Triplex Reel Mower and stared at the newcomer on the field. The dark bird resembled a shadow hovering over the field, but the long coarse legs attached to it did not. Sergio tried to wave to Alayna as she came down the stairs. He wanted to tell her not to do exactly what she was doing, but it was too late. As she started over the wall, Sergio looked back at the Hose Team, watering the dirt around the bases. They were too far away to help. The Toro Triplex roared to life as he steered in a straight line toward his friend. The animal did not move.

Alayna straightened her hair as she began to video the animal. Sergio drove closer, but Alayna waved him off as the livestream began.

"Hey guys! You're never going to believe the special guest we have today at Surprise Stadium!" Repositioning, she ensured the cassowary was visible behind her. "Looks like an ostrich decided it's coming to join us. I know the ostrich festival is going on in Chandler this coming weekend, but this is *not* a PR stunt. This little boy just wandered in to—"

Alayna's eyes grew wide as she watched the video recording her. The bird's head lowered. Its casque pointed forward. Each leg kicked in rapid succession as the animal gained speed. Three seconds later, the casque drilled into Alayna's back. Alayna hit the ground almost twenty feet from where she had been; her iPhone nowhere near her, but still livestreaming, even though viewers only saw the sky.

Sergio screamed for help. The three remaining members of the hose team turned the water on the animal. The lead trying to hold on to the hose, even as his fear overtook him. The animal's feathers hung like soaked horsehair as she cocked her head and stared at Shane Eastman, the man who sprayed her.

Shane dropped the hose and the three men tried to run. The bird was on them immediately. Her beak ripped through the intestines of a man who had only worked there for two weeks. She turned her attention to the next one. Her casque connected with his ribs the same way it had damaged Alayna's spine. Her foot lifted and dropped, ripping through the man's chest. She left him for dead and turned to Shane. As Shane ran, Sergio made his choice.

The three cutting units of the mower roared to life. The two in the front reflected the sun on their steel blades. The one underneath the seat vibrated Sergio's chair lightly as he raised the blades. He knew he could not just run over the bird, but he thought he could save at least part of his crew. As the mower grew closer, the noise drove the bird toward the outfield. The bird moved away from the noise, moving back to the outfield. The distance did not stop her from watching as Shane climbed onto the motor on the back of the mower and the two men drove toward the exit.

Sergio's eyes never left the tunnel as he drove toward it. Shane tapped his shoulder, leaning forward, "She's alive! We have to go back."

"What?"

"Alayna is alive!" Shane shouted.

Sergio looked back over his shoulder and saw Alayna sitting up, leaning forward. He would come back for her. There wasn't room for all three on the mower. He refocused on the tunnel, planning to get the injury cart and return.

But then he saw the cassowary running full bore behind the mower. Her feet connected with the lawn faster with each step. Her head was not lowered this time and Sergio clearly saw her eyes. The pink–white light emitting from them radiated on either side of her narrow mandible.

"What is that thing?" Shane asked.

Pain exploded through his whole body at once as the cassowary's beak ripped through his back just to the left of his spine, piercing his heart from the backside. His ribs shattered as he held eye contact with Sergio. The bird came to a full stop, the lifeless body of her victim skewered on her neck.

Sergio screamed, but knew he had no choice. He had to make it to the tunnel. He refused to look back. He knew the animal was probably right behind him. He managed two Our Fathers and a single Hail Mary before he was in the tunnel. Sergio catapulted himself off the mower and ran down a side hall toward the sectioned area only employees could use. He screamed a blabbering incoherence, but there was no one to hear him. His raspy breath echoed in the hall as he reached for the door.

It was locked.

Squeezing his eyes shut, Sergio moaned, whimpering as his chin and lips trembled. His head shook in denial as he clapped his hands over his ears and crumpled, sinking to the ground. He forced his eyes open, slowly, and found himself completely alone.

Alayna Amaro pulled herself up, but quickly found she could not put any weight on her right ankle. She watched in horror as the cassowary attacked Shane Eastman, stabbing through his back before throwing him through the air. She found herself only fifteen feet from the dugout. If she could make it in there, she could enter the building and find help.

Her heartbeat thrashed in her ears, matching intensity with the pain of each labored breath. The world spun around her as she tried to pull herself across the grass. Clinching her teeth, Alayna expelled a loud grunt as her injured ankle trailed behind her.

She found herself at the entrance to the dugout. Each stair rattled her collapsed lung as she pulled forward, before laying still for a minute to readjust. A low rumble filled the air around her, vibrating the molars at the back of her mouth. It was followed by a deep cooing sound as the cassowary landed in front of her. Its head bobbled with each small noise in the park, but it never broke eye contact.

Tears streamed down Alayna's face as she laughed. She threw out her right arm, grabbing the closest seat in the dug out to pull herself forward. Her laughter grew louder. It turned to screeches of agony as the beak slammed into her hand, separating her tendons and shattering her capitate. Alayna pulled her hand toward her face as her screams turned to whispers. The cassowary jumped straight up, bringing both talons down on Alayna's head.

Alayna's body lay in the dugout for over an hour before Sergio found her. The bird, of course, was nowhere to be found.

PIC
VID

Chapter Nine

Cathy Cakebread exited the metal gate of the Wildlife Preserve. Her heels clicked across the sidewalk as she moved toward the makeshift podium near the guest entryway. The small crowd gathered in the parking lot was comprised mostly, but not entirely, of news crews. Cathy pushed the renegade strands of hair out of her eyes as she adjusted the microphone to the right height and began.

"Yes. Good morning. I'm going to read the official statement and then I'll take questions afterward.

"As everyone is aware, there was an incident at the zoo this morning with one of our animals. I want to share some of the facts about the situation and how we're investigating and the impact it's had on our team.

"At approximately 1:00 AM this morning, one of our keepers was delivering diets to our 13–year-old Southern Cassowary. The cassowary became aggressive and attacked the keeper before escaping from her enclosure. It is with my deepest regrets that I must report that the keeper's injuries were severe and he did not survive the encounter.

"The animal appears to have not only escaped her enclosure, but the property of the Toscano Wildlife Preserve, as well.

"Our animal care, veterinary staff, and security went right into our planned actions for situations like this. Our staff are currently working with local law enforcement to track her and bring the animal back to the property safely and securely. It is, of course, a tragedy to lose a staff member, but I cannot give you more details as next of kin needs to be notified first. I will open this for questions, but please understand that there is a lot I cannot answer until a full investigation has been completed."

Cathy pointed to a young woman from ABC–15. "Yes?"

"Can you describe the enclosure and the barriers in place to prevent this? And does that barrier system meet federal and state guidelines?"

"Yes. It is a two–barrier system, which is almost always the norm when displaying a predator; meaning there is a fence around the enclosure, and then a few feet and another, smaller, fence near the zoo guests, meant to keep them far enough from the animal they cannot be endangered while visiting our preserve. Additionally, we are inspected by the USDA. We receive random inspections to ensure the enclosures and the barrier meet or exceed any regulations they put in place."

"I got a question." A voice boomed from the back, his slight southern accent echoing through the somber crowd. Nicolas James strode forward in a t–shirt that read, "3% MIGHT — 100% RIGHT." He did not necessarily push his way to the front, but his aura seemed to knock people aside.

Cathy watched as he held eye contact with her. "Yes?"

"Does it need to be alive for the reward?"

"Reward?"

"Yeah. If I bring you your bird, what do I get?"

Cathy shook her head slowly side to side. "I do not know. We haven't spoken in those terms." Nicolas stopped four feet in front of the podium, as Cathy added, "And yes, we would prefer the bird is alive. If we decide it needs to be put down, we would do so humanely through our exotic veterinarian on staff."

"You think that would be more humane than me putting it down while it's not caged up?"

"I'm not going to continue this conversation with you. I don't like how—"

His hand shot into the air as he turned to face the crowd.

"Is that what all of you want? Everyone watching at home? You want a murderous bird rampaging through the Valley? Killing your kids because these fuckwads won't take the proper precautions?"

When he saw the crowd wasn't going to take his side, Nicolas James strode back to his pickup. "Well, maybe you guys won't put a stop to this animal, but I sure as hell will. I'll send you the rest of the bird after I mount his fucking head on my wall."

The two flags on the back of the white pickup fluttered as the engine roared to life. A cloud of exhaust shot at the people gathered as Nicolas' middle finger made an encore appearance from the driver's side window. His buddy in back raised a PBR in salute to everyone and pulled a long sip from the can.

Cathy shook her head, looking back at the news crews as Nicolas drove away.

"Any more questions?"

Tobias Keller pulled his empty can to his mouth and drained a trail of tobacco heavy saliva into it. He sucked the air from his closed mouth to his throat as the wad of Skoal repacked around his bottom gum. Gazing out the window, he raised an eyebrow to Nicolas. "We're still gonna find this fucking bird right?"

"You're goddamn right. I got that whole open wall in the basement where Tammy's stuff used to be. I'll stuff this thing and put it over there. Maybe I'll put a fucking saddle on it so my boys have something new to do when they visit every month."

Tobias smiled, his lower lip pressing against his buck teeth as he did so. "Alrighty then. How do we find it?" His eyes went to the Magnum kukri machete behind the driver's seat. Tobias had never seen the seventeen–inch blade in a sheath and wondered if Nicolas even knew where it was. He smiled to himself, as he ran a scenario in his mind where he got to go full ninja on the animal and keep the head as a trophy for himself.

Nicolas ripped a Marlboro Red out of the crumpled pack with his teeth. It was one of only two more before his lucky; still standing tobacco side up. He grunted as his elbow dug into Tobias' arm. Tobias removed the Zippo from his pocket and struck it. Nicolas pulled a long drag as the cherry lit.

Tobias laughed, "That's another seven years."

Emmanuel knocked on the window from the back of the truck. He held up an unopened PBR, water from the cooler running down the sides of the can. Nicolas shook him off, pointing at the steering wheel. "Dumb fuck."

Tobias slid the small cab window open to the bed of the truck. "Let's not be so hasty. I ain't driving." Emmanuel passed him a beer. Tobias spit another mouthful of brown goop into his first can. "Now I just gotta remember which is which."

Nicolas laughed for the first time that day. "Yeah, don't do that again."

Tobias smiled a crooked half smile. "So you gonna tell me how we find this beast?"

Nicolas stared straight ahead as he pulled another long drag off the Marlboro. "Same way we catch anything. We need some bait. Then, when it comes, we blow it to hell."

Kaitlyn stared down at her phone as it rang. She looked up. "It's Cathy."

Jerome shrugged. "She didn't just text?"

"Hello?" Kaitlyn tried to sound cheery, but it proved difficult.

"Kaitlyn. It's me, Cathy. Hey listen. We had a little incident at the press conference. A man in a white pickup interrupted the press conference to tell us he's going to hunt down Cassie."

"What? What do you mean?"

"It was a group of three men who looked like they crawled out of an internet meme. Flags on the back of the pickup, guns at their hips, you know the type. They wanted to hunt her for a reward and then threatened us and left."

"Okay..."

"What is it?" Brungardt asked, scooting as far forward as he could.

Kaitlyn held up a finger to him as Cathy said, "You probably won't have any issues, but I just want you to keep an eye out. Just in case." Cathy swallowed hard as she paused. "I'll screenshot you an updated location in a couple minutes. Call me right away if you find anything."

Less than a mile away, Allie Jo Thompson turned onto a side street in a residential neighborhood, as she decided to take the longer route on her jog to Trader Joe's. Her auburn hair reflected the early morning light, resembling fire against the back of her sports bra. Her hand clenched to her bare abdomen and her large green eyes grew even bigger as she found herself not six feet away from the largest bird she'd ever seen.

The cassowary towered over her by more than a foot. Its long grotesque legs appeared carved from stone. Each toe ended with a talon longer than her hand. Allie Jo took three small steps back. The bird did not move. Glancing around, she saw no vehicles to hide behind; no rocks large enough to provide more than a stepping stone between her and the animal.

The brick wall surrounding the closest property was only a few feet away, but she did not know if she could pull herself over it. Even if she managed, she did not know what to do after that.

She knew she couldn't run. Carefully removing her phone from the pockets of her shorts, Allie Jo dialed nine–one–one. The bird's head appeared to move as the dispatcher answered the call. "*Nine–one–one. What is your emergency?*"

"You know that really big bird that's trending? It's standing in front of me."

"*Excuse me? Ma'am this is—*"

Allie Jo lowered her volume, trying to remain calm, but she wanted to scream at the dispatcher. "That cassowary. The one in the news. He's staring me dead in the eye. Six or seven–foot–tall bird. All black. Blue head. Pink dangly things on its neck. And crazy LED eyes."

"*What is your location?*"

Allie Jo glanced quickly up at the street sign. "I'm at the corner of Mountain View and Parkway."

"*Ma'am, listen to me. That bird is reportedly extremely dangerous. Is there anywhere you can move without startling it?*"

"Not really. I'm going to attempt to just move backward out of the area."

"*Okay. A squad car is only seven blocks from you. Stay on the phone with me.*"

Allie Jo took two more steps back. On the second step, her shoe caught a rock. The rock skidded out from her shoe, shooting into the street. The cassowary let out a low rumble.

"Ah fuck."

"Ma'am? Ma'am, what is happening?"
The bird moved forward quickly, intentionally. Suddenly only a few feet away, it stopped. The animal's wings opened and closed in a show of intimidation. They were smaller than Allie Jo expected.

The bird swung her foot at Allie Jo. The pain was instantaneous, screaming throughout her body. The talon that ripped her abdomen was bigger than Allie Jo's head; the nail at the end of the middle toe slashed one perfectly straight gash from her left side to her right. Her bowels unwound, cascading to the warm pavement around her, her hands unsuccessfully attempting to catch her intestines.

The bird kicked off the ground, jumping onto Allie Jo. The impact knocked her over so quickly her head hit the pavement before Allie Jo understood what happened. Cassie stared down at Allie Jo, opened her mouth, and let out a loud booming sound so loud Allie Jo heard nothing after it. She watched through her tears, unable to fight back, as Cassie's neck swooped down and the bird took a bite.

The cassowary held Allie Jo's small intestine in her mouth for second before she slurped it in like a worm from the ground. Blood flew around her, but Cassie did not seem to mind.

CHAPTER TEN

Fernando Ramos's carefully manicured beard poked into his neck as he stared down at the phone in the spring–loaded mount on the drone's controller. Judging from the latest news reports and what he had seen on Twitter, Fernando thought he knew about where the bird should be. He wanted so badly to find it before anyone else did.

The new drone was not even available on the market yet; Fernando's company had been testing them for the last two weeks. An upgrade to the previous version, this one had almost one–hundred–seventy–five percent the battery life of Fernando's other drones. He knew that might be necessary while tracking the escaped cassowary.

Singing quietly to himself, Fernando waited for the drone to make it the over two miles west of his house. He had no way to know if the bird was still in the vicinity last reported on Twitter. But as the SWAT SUV's, police cars, and news vans came into view on the screen, he knew that, at the very least, other people thought the animal was still there.

The drone straddled the FFA's flight ceiling, hovering four-hundred feet above the area. The DSLR camera scanned the vehicles parked haphazardly through the streets, blocking traffic, but not really creating a scenario where the bird wouldn't be able to get through. Six officers stood approximately eight feet from one another, creating an L–shape as the cassowary watched them from the lawn of the park.

The nine-foot wall behind the animal cut off its only other path of escape. But the cassowary didn't appear to want to escape, as it stood, looking questioningly at the man with outstretched hands, attempting to communicate with his fellow officers.

Cassie's neck craned into an *s* as she quickly moved to pick at some feathers with her beak before returning her attention to the man who believed he was in control of the situation.

Officer Gavin Moore was the last to arrive on the scene. He parked his squad car at the back and sat there for a minute, preparing for the job ahead of him. Reaching over, he moved his dash camera enough to point it toward where the bird stood.

Big fucking bird. They weren't joking about this thing.

It sat on the grass some fifty yards from him and still looked like it took up more room than the St. Bernard his wife decided that they needed the year before. He tapped some keys on the swivel–mounted laptop between the driver and passenger seats before shoving a handful of zip ties into his pocket. He didn't know what he'd use them for but decided he would rather have them ready if need be.

He drew a succession of sips out of the thermos in his cup holder, staring out at his men gathered near the beast.

Moore inhaled once deeply, no longer even recognizing the combination of musty fabric, stale coffee, fried grease, sweat, and sour vomit lingering in the car. He reached back, unlatched his Remington 870 shotgun and joined his crew near the bird.

The cassowary stood at attention. She sank forward slightly, stretching her back as her knees bent. As she rose to her full height, her eyes never left Officer Moore. Those brilliant eyes, radiating an unnatural light around the head of the beast. The animal was larger than any ostrich Moore had seen, but it was the eyes that intimidated the hell out of him; the eyes which kept Officer Moore from reaching for his firearm.

How were they that color? How did they emit that light? How did no one else around him seem to care?

Moore kept his hands outstretched, trying his best to tell the others not to shoot, but it was useless. In Phoenix, when five police officers have their firearms pointed at a target, a bullet is inevitable. The animal took a step back, still not breaking eye contact. All six men moved forward.

But Officer Tyler Reilly did not stop.

Reilly was lost in the brilliant pink light. A soft rumble cascaded through the air as he stepped closer to the cassowary. The intensity of the sound grew until it shook Reilly's rib cage. The bird's head cocked to the left, now staring Reilly in the eye. The man's feet stopped moving, but he did not dare blink, staring at the animal through the sight on the 9mm like he somehow thought this little gun would save him in this fight.

Did this bird just smile?

Officer Reilly couldn't be sure, but part of him believed so. It only made him want to dump a round in the animal even more.

The closer he got, the bigger the cassowary seemed to grow.

"Reilly! Back off." Moore's voice boomed behind him, but Tyler Reilly paid no attention to it. "Reilly! That was a goddamn order. Back off."

As he lowered the gun, the rumble died down a bit.

Is it coming from the fucking bird?

And then it moved.

"LOOK OUT!" screamed Moore, as he finally brought his firearm up.

But the bird didn't attack. She simply began to stroll to the east. Reilly walked parallel to her, a safe six feet away. Or at least he told himself it was safe.

The bird took a step. Reilly took a step. The bird took one. Reilly took one. But no. Because when Reilly stopped, the bird stopped.

Who's following whom?

Reilly turned slowly back to look at Moore and the others. They were following but were more than twenty feet away still. Tyler Reilly could not see it, but the bird moved her head in the same direction. As Reilly turned back to face the cassowary, the bird turned toward him, eye to eye, beak to nose.

Officer Reilly's head pulled back in confusion. The cassowary's head did the same.

The two stared at one another, the bird's dazzling rose–colored eyes almost mesmerizing. Neither moved for a full ten seconds. Reilly took two steps back. The cassowary did the same.

A grumble rolled out of the man's lips as he said, "What in the fuck?"

A rumble grew, reverberating in every direction at once. The light emanating from the eyes became more prominent. The pink fleshy double wattle glowed an intense pink, increasing in color even as Reilly stared at it. The bird's call grew louder.

Reilly turned back to Moore. "You hear that?"

As Reilly turned back, the beak shot forward, ripping through the root of Reilly's nose. The man's entire face shattered at once. Blood emptied from the large hole in Reilly's head as the bird recoiled; chunks of grey meat hung from between the upper and lower mandible of the mouth as the bird swallowed some of the frontal lobe.

"OPEN FIRE!" screamed Officer Moore.

Fernando lowered the drone closer to the scene as the SWAT team and the local police emptied their Remington 870s and Colt M4 Carbines. In a fraction of a second, the cassowary's body slammed into the gravel.

"Hold your fire!" Officer Moore could be heard yelling, even though most were out of ammunition. The grass was torn up from missed shots. Several bullets ricocheted off the cement wall behind the large animal. The cassowary herself was full of entry points and exit wounds, but no blood seemed to leave the body. The lights of the eyes were gone, replaced by black orbs that seemed to absorb any light that touched them.

As Moore drew closer to the fallen animal, the world shifted around him. The sensation of floating overtook him as time stood still and he experienced the ability to see the smallest details. To the left of him dust sifted down from the rafters of an older building. A single shutter hanging on the building slanted askew. The gate in the wall to his right swayed slightly. A guttural roar grew, this time from the earth. A crack appeared in the cement blocks of the wall. The ground shook noticeably as a car alarm down the street began to call. The taste of burning plastic and dust reached the back of Moore's throat, mixing with sour saliva in his mouth.

A dark red light cascaded out of the bird through every hole the rescue team had put into it. The color muted itself, growing brighter, lighter, until it was pink and then almost white. Moore shielded his eyes; the intensity of the light doubling before shooting right back into the bird. Her head rose slowly, her neck extending vertebrae by vertebrae, until she stared into Officer Moore's eyes.

Cassie's own eyes glowed brightly as the bird stood. The earth heaved. Moore was thrown into the wall, his skin scraping the rough cement. Dust sifted down his neck as he threw one arm over his head. He slammed to the ground, choking on dust, biting his lip as he fell. His teeth clattered together with the aftershocks of the hit.

His firearm empty, Moore pointed his taser at the wild animal, knowing it would do no good. His hand trembled so violently the taser fell to the ground beside him as Officer Moore wet himself.

Within thirty minutes of Fernando Ramos loading the video, it went viral. It spread not only through Arizona and the United States, but across the world. And while almost everyone stared with horror watching big bad American men gather around a wild animal and unload way too many rounds into it, it was the rise of the dead that fucked them up.

It was that return to life.

That cascade of brilliant white light with the pink overtones.

The way the bird seemed to magically grow.

It was the screams of the officer on the ground that stuck with viewers hours after they watched the video too many times to count.

It was the slaughter of two members of the SWAT team who tried to run to no avail.

The overturned police car with the door ripped off the hinge and the trail of blood running from the open space.

And it was the eerie silence when the animal walked away from the scene of the crime and the drone rose into the air, leaving the massacre behind.

CHAPTER ELEVEN

AJ Hernandez stared at himself in the mirror as he applied his eyeliner. The electro–white contacts juxtaposed the dark charcoal around his eyes which blended out into hues of crimson and firebrick. He dusted himself one more time, looking at his profile from each angle he could before putting on the killer's mask. The eyeliner added depth to the mask, instantly creating a more menacing look.

In the living room, Allison and Ian rehearsed lines. The weight of the script pressed down on Ian's black jeans as he recited his lines with his eyes closed. Shelly Grant teased and sprayed Allison's hair. A small smirk crossed her face as AJ winked at her from behind the mask as he walked past.

In the kitchen, AJ grabbed two cereal bars off the table filled with snacks. He had been on professional sets with less of a spread, but he gripped his stomach as he looked at most of it. He pushed the cereal bars into his pocket as he pulled a water bottle from the cooler.

The screen door scraped open as AJ stepped onto the patio. He made his way past the table and chairs and the small fire pit and continued out to the set they'd spent all week building. The director, Brian Haas, craned his neck, wedging his cell phone between his shoulder and his ear as he spoke. AJ inhaled the fresh lumber and paint smells as Brian held up all five fingers on his left hand.

Samantha Langdon stood at the far end of the

set, adjusting the white screens suspended above the lights. She was the final girl in the film; the one who would survive. AJ kept his distance from most of the cast to keep a certain reverence of their reactions to his character, but even more so with Samantha. She was the one who needed to buy into his character the most, and as such he tried not to build too much rapport with her. He stood, staring at her from behind the mask and then quickly turned and walked around the house toward the end of the property.

Before each scene, he liked to get time alone and really get into character. *MURDERDOME* was, by no means, a high budget film, but AJ had not been this excited for a role in almost five years. Normally, people cast him as characters closer to his real–life demeanor. He was the good guy. The best friend. The happy guy with great advice.

Not Brian. Brian saw something else in AJ and this time he got to play THE KILLER; a seriously wronged individual hellbent on revenge.

But while it excited AJ, it also gave him headaches and increased the likelihood of ulcers. Channeling the rage and pain the character demanded had affected his sleep the last two weeks. The excessive amount of energy drinks, fast food, and sugary snacks had done a number on his digestive system as well. Pacing back and forth, lost in thought, AJ watched a mix of sun and shadow as light filtered down through the trees overhead.

He pulled THE KILLER's mask up, letting it balance atop his head. As he bit into one of the cereal bars, AJ turned and found himself face to face with a small blue head with piercing salmon colored eyes. The beak opened and immediately closed on AJ's neck, severing the full left side of his head. He had laughed in that final second at the ridiculousness of the situation.

Even in death, AJ Hernandez went out with a smile on his face.

The same could not be said for his friends.

Ian stood, stretching, his pony tail reaching down his back. He lifted a foot to lace his boot on the side of a crate of seemingly random cords. "You ready to do this?"

"Get killed in a horror movie with you? Fuck yeah," Allison laughed.

Ian gave her quick kiss. "I like your hair like this."

"Thanks."

The two made their way out to the set. Allison's eyes traced the tape marks on the floor designating where camera shots should take place. She watched Samantha Langdon rummage through boxes and crates containing gaff tape, lenses, electrical cords, and headsets. The twenty–one–year–old handed Brian a pair of cushioned headphones.

Brian waved, "Hey, Ian! Can you go grab AJ? He went for a walk that way and hasn't come back." He pointed to the far side of the yard, on the side of the house. Ian gave him a thumbs up and moved that direction. Allison followed her husband.

They saw AJ as soon as they turned the corner. The pool of blood outlined his body, his face slumped to one side. The makeup highlighted his smile making it feel even more out of place. Allison screamed. Ian's focus darted around the area looking for anything that could have caused this.

"Go get help." Looking back at his wife, Ian was stunned to see Allison pointing up into the tree, unable to speak.

His eyes followed where she was pointing, and he saw it. The cassowary stared back at him, lying in brooding position on a thick branch almost directly above him; her neck craned in an *S* shape as she looked down at him. A low rumble emitted from the bird, vibrating Ian's chest. His eyes returned to his wife.

"Allison. Look at me. I need you to walk away slowly and go get help."

The bird descended instantly; claws out, beak down. The talons ripped through the muscles in Ian's back, shredding him. His body crumpled under the weight as the cassowary landed and dug into his spine. The beak snapped through the vertebrae without any resistance.

Allison ran as fast as she could, but the animal was on her. She turned the corner of the house, screaming, as the bird jumped toward her. The talons came out again. The long nails dug into her skin and closed into the equivalent of fists. The tendons, muscles, and bones ground to mulch as the bird pecked through Allison's skull several times. Clumps of all three layers of meninges pulled loose. The severed membrane dangled from the savage cassowary's mandibles.

Samantha adjusted the mic as Brian checked the audio. He gave her a thumbs up. "We're good to go. Thanks for your help."

"No problem." She pulled her hair into a ponytail. "Is that about how everything looked in the last take yesterday?"

"That's it. Looks great."

A primal scream ripped through the air. Brian and Sam watched as Allison turned the corner of the house. The animal following her was unlike anything Samantha had ever seen; larger than an ostrich with deep black feathers, long reptilian legs, and some sort of weird growth on top of its head. Before she could register what she was looking at, the bird tackled Allison to the ground and rapidly attacked her skull.

Pieces of brain stuck to the bird's mouth as Brian screamed, "Get the fuck out of here!"

Samantha tried to navigate the uneven footing as she dodged the cords running across the ground. Once on the grass they made a dash directly for the back door of the house. The animal was almost on them as Brian threw open the door to wave Samantha in. He ducked down, plucking a sun–bleached garden gnome from the patio. He launched the gnome, which exploded on the bird's beak. The animal barely seemed to notice.

As they ran into the kitchen, Shelly smiled brightly holding up her phone. "You'll never believe what I just saw on Twitter. This bird—"

"Not now, Shelly!" Brian locked the door, well aware it would make no difference as Sam ran into the living room, past Shelly. Brian grabbed Shelly's hand. "We gotta go. Now."

Shelly turned back as the cassowary burst through the door. "What the *fuck* is that?" She looked back down at her phone, her eyes growing larger. "Oh shit."

The bird's neck swung to the side and arced back in one quick motion. Shelly slammed into the wall but regained her footing. She tried to follow her friends, but the bird kicked straight sideways. Shelly's face crunched against the wall. A trail of blood marked her descent to the floor. The cassowary drilled its beak through the top of Shelly's head. Cassie stood, admiring her work, and then followed the other two.

Brian started up the stairs, but Samantha pulled his shirt to stop him, "What are you doing? No one survives running upstairs. It's a cardinal rule."

"Trust me" Brian kept going. "We know she can go through doors. We don't know if she can take stairs!" Samantha looked back at Shelly and then the cassowary. She ran up the stairs.

On the second floor, Brian ran to the recessed entryway to the attic. Jumping twice, he was able to grab the latch and pull it open. The cassowary roared from below, the sound almost echoing the canned dinosaur sounds Samantha had heard too many times at the Natural History Museum in Mesa.

The wobbly wooden ladder dropped. Brian motioned for Samantha to climb. She pursed her lips, lowering her brows. Lifting her chin, she made slow, cautious movements to climb.

"Let's go." Brian was right behind her, forcing her to move more quickly.

Samantha pulled herself over the top. The stench of stale air, sawdust and mildew attacked her senses. She breathed into her elbow trying to fight the urge to sneeze. Everything seemed a shade of brown, from the unfinished construction to the plywood to even the totes piled in an organized manner. Cardboard boxes held newspapers, books, and random papers. The brown tint turned into a sepia tone as it mixed with a pink hue shining from below. Motes of dust danced in the rays of light.

Brian's arms flailed as he tried to pull himself up the ladder. The cassowary jumped underneath him, nipping at his feet. Brian froze. His eyes squeezed shut. He refused to look.

"No. No. No. No. No." His palm tapped the dusty floorboards. His back arched. A scream erupted from his throat as his neck tightened. The beak locked around his ankle yanked back. Blood shot out as his ankle ripped away. The bottom portion of his fibula shattered. The ligaments pulled free. Brian screamed several more times as the bird bit rapidly, severing muscles in Brian's foot.

With one last thrust, he cleared the hatch, collapsing on the floor near a pile of mouse droppings. Samantha tugged on the ladder, pulling it up. The cassowary jumped repeatedly, pecking at Samantha's hands, but missing. Samantha slammed the hatch shut as Brian rolled to the side, tears running down his face. She ran to the closest pile of totes, grabbing the one that looked the heaviest. She pulled it on top of the hatch.

Wiping tears from his cheeks, Brian pointed her to another tote where she found some old t–shirts that no longer fit him. He ripped one into pieces, creating a tourniquet for his ankle. The two of them listened in near silence, waiting for the cassowary to come back, but heard nothing.

Brian flattened his palm against the floorboards as he tried to brace himself. With his full weight on his wrist, he pushed himself into a more comfortable seated position.

Samantha pointed to the window. "What about that way?"

Brian whispered back. "It drops to the balcony. I can't make that leap. Maybe you can, but I think we're safer staying right here." His fingers split further apart as he leaned more of his weight on his wrists. "We have to figure out—"

The cassowary's beak ripped through the floor and exited through the top of Brian's hand. His shrill scream antagonized the beast and the cassowary's beak opened and closed rapidly, severing every muscle and tendon. The beak disappeared, but shards of wood remained in the wound. Pushing one eye shut, Brian turned away from the damage. His teeth ground together as he pulled his hand free. Blood poured down his arm as he screamed.

The sound was followed by the bird's beak slamming into the floor of the attic several times. New holes appeared less than two feet from Brian. The floorboards shook. The full weight of the bird hit below the shattered flooring with each jump.

"We gotta fucking go!" screamed Samantha.

A talon rose through one of the holes. The cassowary gripped the side of a support beam and began her ascent into the room, pushing the attic floor out of her way with the casque on her head.

Brian's hand poured blood as he pointed to the window. "Go!"

Samantha stopped at the window; the sill covered in dead flies. She looked back at Brian. "I'm sorry, I'll get help!" She threw the window open as the cassowary broke through the floor.

The bird landed, stretching as though waking from a nap. Her focus locked on the man lying in front of her. She took a step forward, as the floor shook and crackled with her weight. Her foot reached forward, and she took another step. As her weight shifted, the floor gave way. Cassie's beak shot forward, skewering Brian in the neck.

Screaming silently, Brian was pulled through the floor.

Gone forever.

CHAPTER TWELVE

"I'm Hunter Womack and this is *Channel 3 Eyewitness* news. Social media is blowing up with the cassowary that has been running rampant through the West Valley this morning. A minimum of six people are dead and at least two of those deaths have gone viral on social media channels."

"I don't like that." Liz interrupted, lowering the camera. "You said social media twice. That's just not working for me."

Hunter shot back, "You know what's not working for me? Constantly running after this bird and arriving too late. The fact that everything is viral before I can even talk about it on the air."

"That's the world we live in, Hunter. Information is outdated before it's even reported."

"And that's why no one takes us seriously. We're literally called *Eyewitness News*, but we're not witnessing anything. How do we get ahead of it? That's our only hope. We have to be there when news occurs."

Liz started walking toward the van.

Hunter called after her, "What? Was it something I said? Where are you going?"

Liz smiled. "Let's go, Mr. Eyewitness News. We're not going to get ahead of this bird by parking here talking about things everyone else already watched on Twitter. We need to get on the road."

Hunter jogged toward the van. "Okay! Let's do it." As he pulled his seatbelt across his chest, Hunter smiled. "Any idea where we go next?"

Liz shook her head, as a laugh escaped. "Nope."

"So what's the plan?"

"Wait for social media to tell us where to go."

Kevin Lewis stared intently at the footage on his phone in disbelief. Had he seen what he thought he had? Fucking hell.

He stood up and returned KJ to his terrarium. "Sorry dude. I'll be back soon. Don't fucking go anywhere. And if you do, just don't go outside, okay?"

He sent a single text to his nephew Jerome.

Kevin: J. Michael Where you at?

The pickup turned back onto the major parkway, both flags waving in the wind as Nicolas hit the gas midway through the turn. Emmanuel gripped the siderail of the truck as he wiped a drop of PBR off his shirt collar with his other thumb.

In the cab, Tobias sat quietly, his hand to his mouth, index finger across his lips like it would stop him from saying something he would regret. Nicolas James hadn't spoken since they had heard the news report on the radio involving the police and the cassowary.

Tobias watched as Nicolas opened his pack of cigarettes and pulled the second to last one out with his teeth. Leaning over, Tobias lit it for him without saying a word.

Nicolas drew a drag and let it exit through his nose before raising an eyebrow and mumbling, "What? No joke about me owing you part of my sex life?"

Tobias shrugged. "I didn't wanna push it right now."

96

Nicolas' eyebrows squished as he smirked.

"Oh, I'm not mad. The cops didn't finish the job, right? So, it's still out there. If anything, I should be excited. It'll make me look like even more of a bad ass when I kill the damn thing."

A smile slowly split Tobias' beard. "That's the spirit. So where are we heading?"

"Exactly where those dumbass cops were. It's gotta be near there. We're gonna find it. It couldn't have gone too far."

Nicolas pulled the pickup into a residential area. Holding his hand out, he mumbled, "Alright. Let me see this damn video again."

Tobias pushed play on Fernando's drone footage. As they watched, the two men laughed.

"Look at this stupid fuck. These supposedly trained law enforcement bitches can't handle an overgrown chicken and we wonder why crime is so out of control in Phoenix."

Tobias laughed. "Oh shit. The bird is just imitating him!"

As the bird's beak ripped through Officer Reilly's face, Tobias and Nicolas both audibly gasped.

"God *damn*!" Nicolas made the second word last three times as long as it should have. "That's one way to go out!"

Tobias absentmindedly tugged Nicolas' sleeve as he pointed toward a girl in the street. "What do you make of this?"

Nicolas eyed Tobias' hand, but let it go, locking eyes on the young woman running toward them waving frantically. Her gaunt frame gave way to smooth toned legs. Her straight brown hair waved behind her with each step.

"Hey! Hey!" She yelled. "Help me! Please! They're all dead!"

Tobias was not happy when he was demoted to the back of the pickup so the pretty girl could have his seat. Emmanuel did not seem pleased to share his leg room, but he was fine with sharing his weed and alcohol, so before long, neither of them cared about much of anything.

Up front, Samantha relayed everything she could think of from the large black bird slaughtering her friends to hiding in the house until it found them there. Brian's death. Her eventual escape through the window and down the roof.

"Do you got a phone?"

Sam slapped her pockets. "No. I must've left it on set." A sense of dread creeped over her as these words left her mouth, her eyes roaming to the three firearms and the large machete behind the driver's seat.

Nicolas pulled the truck into drive as the doors locked. *Way to fucking go, Sam. Just panic and jump in a truck with some guy with a fucking armory in his backseat. That'll turn out fine.*

But things were no better outside the truck. That bird was out there and she knew it.

Nicolas reached for his own phone, driving with his knee. He typed the letters one by one, pausing to search for each one. Google corrected his spelling and he clicked Images.

"This the bird?"

Samantha nodded slowly, thoughtfully. "Yeah, only way bigger. Probably. Hard to tell here, but this one was crazy muscular and had raging hot pink eyes. And it was..." she swallowed, trailing off. She looked at the floor. "You know. Covered in blood."

Nicolas tried not to laugh at this. *Poor stupid girl,* he thought. "Well, you're with the right people now. You'll be safe with us. Ain't no way that thing is gonna get the best of us."

Through the small window, Tobias called, "Nicolas is a certifiable shooting champion. One of the best trophy hunters the state of 'zona ever saw. You wanna see pics?"

Sam did not know what to say so she just agreed. Tobias popped up an app and scrolled through Nicolas' pictures. The deer carcasses didn't bother her much. Her mother and uncles were all avid hunters, but the picture of Nicolas holding up a dead lion by the mane got to her.

Tobias put his phone down as Nicolas said, "Do you know which direction the animal went?"

Samantha pointed the direction she ran from "It went that way, so I came this way."

The pickup started rolling in that direction as Nicolas smiled to Samantha. "Stop worrying, girl. You're safe now."

Sam did not think she'd ever heard words ring as hollow as those, but she figured it was better than taking her chances alone as long as the cassowary was still out there.

Kaitlyn pointed to the picture Cathy sent, where the tracker showed the cassowary inhabiting a small manmade forest on the edge of the Glendale–Surprise border.

"Why can't she just give us the tracker so we could use it in real time?"

Jerome pulled the truck and trailer to the south side of the area. "You know why. Bureaucratic bullshit. Cassie should be in this area," he said, pointing directly next to Kaitlyn's finger. "See those rocks over there? I think that's what this is."

Thomas mumbled, "That's what she just said."

Jerome shot back, "So, what's the plan?"

Brungardt readied a tranquilizer dart and put it into the DJI Dart Gun. "I'm thinking we take different sides. Flank it. Then drive it toward one another."

"I like it, but if we end up in the middle of those trees, how do we get her in the trailer?"

Kaitlyn shrugged. "We'll just drive as close as we can and work from there."

Brungardt shook his head. "That won't be necessary. I've had to tranq Cassie a few times. She doesn't go down instantly. We'll open a path so the only way she can go is toward the Jeep and then we'll figure it out based on how close she gets to the trailer." He smiled as he opened the door. "Don't overthink it."

"Wait." Jerome said. "Do you really think we should split up?"

"One of the best hunting methods in the wild is the way animals surround their prey. Even velociraptors did it. You send one out to distract, while the others ambush from the sides. I know you're a little scared, so I'll let you stay with Kaitlyn."

Brungardt smiled to Kaitlyn. "Do your best to keep him safe. He needs all the help he can get."

The rock quickly gave way to desert flora. The weeping growth of Willow Acacia hung low, covering tumbleweeds, mesquite bushes and desert broom. Thick stemmed yellow and green grass randomly tangled around the toes of his shoes as Brungardt walked. Only the aloe spears appeared to be have been placed with purpose. Thomas' hand scraped against the thorny shrubs as he pushed through.

Pebbles skittered across the ground as he moved, the only real sound aside from the occasional moan of the wind. A small lizard ran to the top of a wind–weathered rock, possibly evading the human intruder; or examining him.

Grit and dust covered his tongue as Thomas quietly wished he had brought some water along.

Nicolas James parked the pickup only a block away, watching the three zoo employees from a distance. The man and woman in the distance disappeared, but he could see the other walking by himself.

"You see that? If they're here, the bird is here. You know they have advanced equipment helping them stalk this thing."

Tobias called from the window. "Oh shit, I know that guy!"

Nicolas's head pulled back as he grimaced. "What do you mean you know him? You two go to Homosexuals Anonymous together or something?"

"I don't *know him* know him. I just know who he is. I was looking at the Preserve's website. See?" Tobias slid his phone through the window to Nicolas.

Nicolas scanned the pictures on the employee page of the Toscano Wildlife Preserve. "Dr. Thomas Brungardt, huh? Well you don't go sending a doctor out unless the bird is there, and it's hurt. This is my chance."

Nicolas pulled the keys from the ignition and smiled to Samantha. "You're gonna be fine, but I want you to stay here. No sense in going head to head with the bird again, right?"

Sam shook her head, "I have no desire to do that."

"Just hang out here and we'll be back shortly." He grabbed one AR–15 and handed the other to Tobias. He pointed at Emmanuel. "Stay here with her."

Tobias smiled, "What? He doesn't get to take a turn?"

Nicolas raised one eyebrow, "Take a turn? What are you gonna fuck her now?"

Tobias spit another stream of tobacco. "I'll fuck her if I want. She ain't gonna put up a fight when she sees these good looks. Maybe I'll fuck her, then put a bullet in her head, and then fuck her again."

Nicolas hit him on the back of the head. "Knock it off. You want to stand around and shoot the shit or get moving and shoot some shit?"

The two walked toward the trees as Emmanuel slid back to the floor of the pickup and started rolling a joint.

Chapter Thirteen

Sun City West, a community on the western end of the Phoenix metropolitan area, was home to more than twenty–five thousand senior citizens, at least seasonally. Nicknamed snowbirds, retirees across the nation flocked to the small town each winter to escape the cold of their home states and find a different kind of warmth with anyone and everyone that they could before they went back to their other lives.

Donald Guillory was especially popular in the tight community, as he was one of the only black men in a city that was primarily Caucasian.

He sat at his kitchen table smoking his after–breakfast Cuban before his daily swim. He flicked ashes with one hand and scrolled through his texts with the other. Two of his favorite ladies each invited him over later in the afternoon.

Rose was a couple years younger than Don. Her energy and enthusiasm never died down. Sometimes she was a bit too much to handle, particularly in public, where her lack of volume control embarrassed him. Still, Don loved putting that endless energy to work in the bedroom... or on her couch... or wherever else he could. He planned on meeting her in the afternoon.

Don: Gotta get home by seven to video chat with the grandkids. Can I come sooner?

He giggled at his own inuendo as he pulled a long drag from the Cuban, rolling the smoke in his mouth. He flicked the ashes again, reaching the end of the cigar as his phone vibrated. He crushed it out before reading

Rose: Of course, honey. You can come any time you want Haha

Don: ;) Pool time. Talk soon, Mamacita.

Don stretched, standing up for the first time since he had started breakfast. He finished his coffee as he prepared a mojito. He gripped a large butcher's knife to slice his limes. The knife was too big for what he needed, but it was out, and he did not want more dishes.

The phone vibrated again. He licked the fingers on his left hand before grabbing the phone. The right hand squeezed the lime into the glass as he read a message from his other beauty.

Sophie: 8 works great. Can't wait to see you tonight. Off to golf.

Sophie: Going to play with these little white balls until I can play with your chocolate monster.

She followed that text with a smiley as Don laughed to himself.

He dropped his bathrobe at the backdoor. Sophie was more refined than the others. She loved great wine, expensive bourbon, cigars, and lying in bed telling stories of her many worldly travels. She regaled him with random facts, and he explained the historical context of the buildings and artifacts she'd seen during her excursions.

If he had to pick just one woman in Sun City West, it would have been Sophie in a heartbeat, but lucky for Don he did not have to limit himself with such choices.

The sun warmed his naked body as Don slid the glass door closed. He smiled to himself, rereading Sophie's words. He did not look up as he moved toward the pool, his foot barely missing the goggles laying out from the day before. The towel in his hand slid into a sun damaged lawn chair as he kicked off his flip–flops. His bare foot scraped the gritty wet concrete, but Don thought nothing of it as he lowered himself into the sun–dappled water, unaware that he was not alone. Resting back in the corner of the pool, his legs floating under him as he sipped his mojito and thought about the things he would do to each woman in the coming hours.

His eyes closed. He pushed his lower back against the bubbling push of water near a pool jet. Don inhaled deeply, stretching his lower back. The sun–warmed stone and earth around him mixed with the mint from the mojito and the chlorine in the air. The sun beat down on him as only the Arizona sun can, warming his skin against the cool water of the pool.

In only a few more months, direct sunlight like this would burn like the fires of hell. For now, his easy smile grew into a yawn. "I might need a nap before I get in their beds."

As he opened his eyes, Don stared at the two bright eyes staring back at him from across the water. They appeared to be attached to a giant floating penis, its hot pink testicles resting on the water while the electric blue shaft led to some sort of rock cap just above the eyes. "What the *fuck*?"

At the sound of his voice, the phallic object turned to the side, allowing Don to make out a beak a few inches long. The pink light glowed more brightly from this angle.

It's a bird?

The question itself increased his body temperature, his heartrate rising. His elbows pressed into his side as he pushed himself back into the wall of the pool. His eyes stared under the penis bird, trying to make sense of the giant black shadow on the water. That is not a shadow, that's the rest of the bird. His toes curled, gripping at the pebbly surface at the bottom of the pool.

"This is... uh... this is a private pool. Can I help you?"

The bird never broke eye contact, its head moving erratically with each gurgle of the filtration vents and every movement of the fronds of the palms above them. The water reflected a mixture of sunlight and the glow of the bird's eyes. The periscope–like neck craned up as the bird began to surface. The full bird came into view, its back appearing to be covered in wet dog hair rather than feathers. A low rumble resonated across the water, creating additional ripples on the surface. The elderly man felt it inside his bones and knew it was time to move but feared what any sudden movement might trigger.

Don slid against the wall slowly, never looking away from the mammoth sized chicken. As he neared the stairs, he shifted his body weight, but still held eye contact. His calf muscle tightened as he pushed off the first stair, his body raising a few inches from the water. He turned, his second foot connecting with the next stair as he pulled himself up more. As he moved to take the next stair, Don became acutely aware of how unprotected his own penis was. THE MONSTER, as Sophie called it, glistened in the sunlight and the elderly man wondered if the bird was holding eye contact or staring at a tasty morsel.

He backed his way out of the rest of the pool, his feet grinding against the pool deck as he moved toward the nearby wall. His outstretched hand found the telescopic pole; the leaf skimmer tightened to the end. As Don removed it from the wall, the cassowary verbally accepted Don's challenge and pulled itself out of the water to meet him head on.

The sound that echoed through the walls of the backyard were a combination of a growl, a roar, and a coo. It rose, landing on the cool deck with a thud. The large talons of each foot stretched in three different direction; the middle nails at least eight inches long, curling to razor sharp points. The scales on the feet were crusty and hard, like something from a bygone era that should not be alive, let alone standing poolside in a man's backyard.

The cassowary lowered her head, her casque aimed right at Don's center, but the man gripped the telescopic pole like a javelin, keeping distance between the bird and himself, as his feet shuffled toward the door.

Each step he took backward was met with a forward step by the large animal. Don's left hand quivered as he reached back for the door handle. As the door slid open, the cassowary's head swung to the side and back, connecting with the pole; one half shattered and flew through the air. Don held the broken half as he watched the pool skimmer crashed to the ground some seven feet away. Don jabbed the remains of the pole at the bird.

The cassowary's head shot forward, her beak slamming into Don's forearm. The scream that ripped through his throat terrified himself more than the bird, but the cassowary took a step back anyway. Don's jaw clenched, his teeth grinding together as his eyes watered. His back arched as though he could run from the pain. He refused to look as his muscles cramped and tightened.

The bird took another step back. Don turned, running for the door. Clearing the threshold, Don pulled the door closed behind him and locked it in one quick motion. He grabbed a nearby towel and applied pressure to the wound. His left foot bounced as a pained hiss escaped his lips. His stomach responded to the aroma of bacon and coffee still thick in the air, but long since gone.

Clutching the towel in his hand, he was semi-relieved to find he still had control of all five fingers. He quickly walked through the kitchen, but the phone was not on any of the stainless steel appliances, the granite counters, or even the small table where he ate most of his meals alone. He grabbed a butcher's knife with his good hand, as though this would somehow save him, and stared out the back door.

There, next to his half-finished mojito, sat his cell phone. "Shit." The sound of his own voice sent goosebumps up his arm as he looked out the door.

The cassowary was nowhere to be seen. "No one is ever gonna believe this shit... and I didn't even get a picture." He started toward the door and abruptly stopped. "I am not falling for that shit." He set the knife down and plucked his keys from their spot on the wall. He took one more look outside.

Maybe it's gone? Maybe it was never really here? Nah. Screw that. I'm out of here.

He turned away to get clothes and leave. A low rumble bellowed behind him, shaking the glass. The walls moved like one of the earthquakes he had experienced living in Southern California. He didn't want to look, but his head turned anyway.

The bird just stood there. Right by the door. It stared at him, eyes glowing, the light reflecting in the panes of the sliding glass. Don knew what was coming. He needed to move, but his feet would not go.

The animal took three steps back, holding eye contact. Her head dropped ever so slightly.

It lunged forward.

The glass door shattered instantly, spidering out from the point of contact. The cassowary's head had gone through, but her body was still outside. The beak opened to a perfect diamond as the bird shrieked like a banshee. Then the head was gone.

Don tried to run as the bird hit the window with its full weight. Shards of glass no bigger than a quarter inch peppered the air, raining down on the bird in slow motion.

One large dinosaur foot hit the linoleum and then the other followed. The nails on the end of each clawed at the tile as the bird opened its small wings in a show of intimidation, spreading as the quill–like feathers pointed directly at Don. He turned, running into the living room, but the bird was on him.

Stretching over the back of the couch, the bird slammed its beak directly into the right side of Don's neck. A jettison of blood sprayed the throw pillows. Don collapsed immediately, the towel in his hand unraveling. The bird stood over him, looking down, its eyes ablaze. Don wanted to kick up at his adversary but had no energy to do so and knew that it would do no good anyway. The bird stared down at Don's naked body.

The beak shot down twice in rapid succession, tearing through his scrotum and picking his 'black berries.' As the bird swallowed, it raised a talon over Don's throat and dropped it quickly, severing the old man's head like a guillotine.

CHAPTER FOURTEEN

Samantha had not heard everything, but she had heard enough to think Tobias planned to rape her, kill her, and then rape her corpse. She knew she needed to escape, and she had to do it right now. She glanced back at Emmanuel just as he licked the rolling paper, her trembling hand fumbling for the door handle.

Her eyes squeezed shut as her body tightened, her teeth chattering like a cold winter day. Her rapid breathing grew as her fingers found the silver door handle. Samantha inhaled one deep, clearing breath and opened her eyes.

BAM! BAM! BAM!

Emmanuel pounded on the window to the cab. Samantha turned slowly, her chin falling to her chest, her rigid posture sagging. She raised her eyes slowly, afraid of what she would see.

Emmanuel looked back at her through his bloodshot eyes. A soft smile split the beard that desperately needed trimming. His right arm reached through the pass through window, and he held an unopened Pabst Blue Ribbon right by Samantha's face.

"I don't have any water," he said. "But if you want this, you can have it."

"No. No, thank you."

Emmanuel shifted his weight. "Okay then." As he did so, he stumbled, the beer can and his hand rubbing against Samantha's chest.

Her lip curled as she swallowed uncomfortably. She pushed his hand away as he fumbled an apology.

"That was an accident. I'm sorry." He smiled. "If I meant to do it, I would've done a way better job." The compulsion to flee overtook her, but she was not sure she could outrun him.

Samantha looked around the inside of the pickup. She tried to hide her glee when she saw the machete Nicolas kept behind his seat.

"You're good. Sorry. I'm just really jumpy." She said, turning more fully toward Emmanuel. "You know what, I think I will take that beer, if you're still offering." Her fingers gripped the handle of the machete as she prepared for the only swing she would get.

As Emmanuel reached through the window the black steel blade buried itself in his arm. It didn't severe the whole arm the way Sam had envisioned it. The two sat staring at one another as the man screamed.

Samantha threw open the door as Emmanuel tried to pull his arm back out of the cab of the pickup, the machete catching on either side of the small window.

"Fucking bitch!" He reached in with his left hand and removed the kukri blade as quickly as he could, blood pouring onto the upholstery. He threw off his jacket, screaming again as the fabric ran over his mutilated arm. He quickly tried to turn the jacket into a tourniquet as he watched Samantha bolt, rushing away from him and away from the trees.

Holding the jacketed arm close to his chest, Emmanuel grabbed a rifle, and fired in Samantha's general direction. His impaired depth perception and tunnel vision did not help his cause. The world appeared to spin around him as he took another shot.

Samantha changed course, charging into the

trees. Emmanuel hooted and hollered every English swear word he could think of and most of the ones he knew in Spanish, thinking at the very least Nicolas would hear him and realize something had gone terribly wrong.

Kaitlyn pointed left. "I'm going to go that way. I want you to keep on this trail. If you see her, just—"

"Why don't we just stay together?"

"So, we find her faster."

Jerome moved closer, only a foot way, smiling. "I'm just saying I'd rather stay with you. Do this together. You and me."

Kaitlyn took a step back. "We need to find Cassie soon. It's been hours. Someone else will find her if we don't. Maybe we should check social media or—"

Jerome was closer. His hand slid to the small of her back. His chest didn't touch hers, but one big breath and they would have. His head tilted. His lips touched hers.

Kaitlyn's arm shot up, covering her chest. Her elbow connected with Jerome's sternum "What the fuck?"

Jerome stumbled back, an incredulous stare haunted his eyes. Three seconds later, he was able to mask it again. "Sorry, I guess I just thought that—"

She threw her arms out. "That what? That we're at work and we're looking for a bird that is murdering people, so maybe we should fuck out in the woods?"

"You're right. I'm sorry. That wasn't the right time."

Kaitlyn's entire head sunk forward in disbelief and astonishment. Her lips opened, but nothing came out at first. "The right time?"

"Just forget it." Jerome turned and started down the trail. Kaitlyn stood watching him go, wrestling with an apology. She had not meant to upset him.

Me? *Upset him? What the fuck is wrong with me? Who the hell cares if he's upset?* Kaitlyn turned left and stormed into the trees.

A small dust devil whipped in the distance, momentarily catching Dr. Brungardt's attention. It was only two feet in diameter and seven feet tall. He watched through the trees as it whipped and turned, particles of dust and debris running in circles with nowhere to go. He wondered if the cassowary was standing nearby watching the dust devil as well.

Of course, in Australia they're called Willy Willies, he thought, slightly annoyed there was no one nearby to tell this piece of useless trivia to.

Suddenly, there was someone nearby. Dr Brungardt heard voices.

"I swear to motherfucking god, if you had hit my shoe with that shit, I will shoot you myself." Nicolas' voice was not raised but it carried authority.

Dr. Brungardt could not see the man speaking, but he saw Tobias, smiling as he looked side to side. "Would you have me stuffed and put in your basement with the others?"

Nicolas took two steps closer to Tobias. "Chewing is disgusting. How do you even do that?" Now that he could see both men, Dr. Brungardt was positive he did not want to spend time getting to know either one.

Tobias pulled another pinch out of the tin, placed it between his lip and his gum and smiled, "Fresh leaf tastes way better than those Marlboros you carry around. And I'm not sucking a stick if you get my meaning."

"Your joke was so well disguised I almost missed it. Can we just go look for this fucking bird already? I'd like to get to it before anyone else does."

The two men moved forward less than fifteen

steps when Tobias pointed into the underbrush. "What's that? Over there?"

"A dust devil, you moron. What are you, new to Arizona?" Nicolas slapped Tobias on the shoulder with disdain.

"Oh baby. You know I like it rough."

"Not that. There. In the bushes."

Dr. Brungardt knew logically that Cassie was too big to hide in the bushes, but he also knew cassowaries were willing to hide almost anywhere.

Nicolas readied his gun. "We'll find out in a second. Ready? Aim!"

Brungardt stumbled out into the open. "Oh shit, sorry. I didn't mean to scare you guys."

Nicolas lowered his weapon, but Tobias kept his pointing toward the sky just in case he wanted to use it quickly. He spit out another trail of tobacco. "Can I help you with something, Dr. Brungardt?"

Thomas froze at the sound of his name. He even pronounced it correctly. Half his friends did not pronounce it correctly. His lower lip pulled into the upper one as Dr. Brungardt let out a long sigh, watching a small rabbit duck out from the bushes.

Are you fucking kidding me?

"Doc, we're gonna need you to tell us where that bird is."

"I mean, that's the issue, right?" Dr. Brungardt shrugged. "If I knew where she was for sure, I'd have already loaded her up and taken her out of here."

Nicolas cracked his neck as he raised his weapon level with Dr. Brungardt's chest. "Drop the weapon."

"It's not a gun. It's a—"

"I know what it is. I didn't ask. I told you to drop it. So do it or I'll drop you."

Dr. Brungardt slowly lowered the dart gun to the ground and took two steps back from it. No one asked him to, but he saw it in so many movies he assumed it was the next step. Nicolas motioned with his head. Tobias took a few steps forward and grabbed the tranquilizer gun. "Hey this is nice."

Nicolas ignored him. "Where are the others?"

"What others?" Brungardt said. "And how do you know my name?"

"Tobias here found you on the zoo's webpage. Where are the two you came here with?"

"Looking for the bird. Same as me."

Nicolas moved closer, staring at the ground, before looking Dr. Brungardt in the eye. "So, where is he?"

"Who?"

"The bird."

"Oh, Cassie is a girl. I didn't realize you—"

Nicolas' fist ricocheted off Dr. Brungardt's jaw. "I don't give a fuck if your cassowary is a transgendered emu. Cut the bullshit and tell me where the fuck it is."

Brungardt rubbed his face. His smile was completely gone. "We seriously don't know. The last update we got, she was supposed to be here. Clearly I haven't found her yet."

"Give me your tracker."

"We don't have a tracker."

"Of course, you have a tracker. Why wouldn't you have a tracker?"

"The Wildlife Preserve didn't hand it out. They kept it there and send us updates now and then."

Nicolas turned back to Tobias, who stood stroking his beard. "Do you believe this piece of shit, Toby?"

Tobias drained a long mucousy trail of chewed tobacco down from his mouth, aiming for a small flower in the middle of the dirt they stood on. The goop hit the flower dead on, pushing it to the ground. Tobias smiled; some tobacco remnants stuck to the front of his teeth.

"You know what? Let's say I do. But that would mean they get the updates somehow, so I'm gonna guess a cell phone. So how about you hand it over?"

Dr. Brungardt reached into his pocket, very slowly removing the phone. His eyes did not leave the trigger finger Nicolas held on the gun in his hand. Tobias held his hand out. Brungardt saw no other options and handed his phone over.

"Let's get the others," Nicolas said, matter-of-factly, as though Dr. Brungardt couldn't hear him.

"Well, they might have left. We were talking about different areas that—"

Nicolas' arm wrapped around Dr. Brungardt's neck in one motion. His strong biceps cut directly into Brungardt's windpipe. The grip tightened with the strength of a king snake, which is pound for pound the strongest snake in the world.

Goddamn it, Thomas. Focus.

"I know you're out there!" Nicolas yelled. "If you don't come out right now, I'm gonna blow this motherfucker's brains all over the place. Then I'm going to come find you."

Samantha bolted from the pickup with no clear destination in mind, just the general idea of nowhere near Emmanuel and nowhere near that giant bird. Her hand swept at the sweat pouring off her face as she stumbled slightly. She caught her balance as the first shot hit the ground near her.

He's trying to shoot me!

More shots peppered the ground in her direction. She needed cover. She turned course, running directly into the trees. About ten feet in, she saw a large rock and climbed behind it. Her ankle throbbed. She rubbed it wondering if she had twisted it without even realizing.

Waiting, she squeezed her eyes shut and

just listened. Emmanuel's manifesto of profanity eventually came to an end. She swiped at her cheeks and forehead repeatedly, wiping off more sweat and some tears she did not realize she had cried. A montage of the encounters of the last hour poured through her head. *None of it's real. This has to be a dream. There's just no way.*

She heard Nicolas' voice and then Tobias'. Crawling from behind the rock, but careful not to stand up, she tried to see what they were doing. As the two came closer to her, Tobias seemed to point right at her.

"There. In the bushes." Samantha's eyes grew large and she managed to turn and crawl away from them. They had seen her, she was sure of it.

Samantha did not move while they spoke to the third man who walked up. She could not make out most of what they said. She was too busy running scenarios in her mind that all ended with her not making it home that night.

Chapter Fifteen

A low, hoarse growl ripped through the air. It took a second for Kaitlyn to recognize it as human. She moved quickly but cautiously as she ventured toward it. She ran in the direction of the voice, her feet bouncing down the trail in rhythm.

Pushing branches out of her way, she saw a man lying on the ground twenty feet from her. His neck stretched as he tried to look up to her.

"Kaitlyn! Help!" Jerome's voice shook with panic. Her feet ground to a halt as she saw him. Jerome lay on the ground, one foot seemed to bend backwards. His arms wrapped around his stomach. The breathing sawed back and forth through his chest. He jolted, as if an invisible pain tore through his back.

Kaitlyn knelt next to Jerome. "What happened?"

Unclenching his jaw, Jerome swallowed hard. His words escaped through labored breaths as he flinched at the slight touch of Kaitlyn's hand.

"Cassie. She came out of nowhere." He tried to sit up, but Kaitlyn told him not to. "She charged. Hit me right here." He pointed to the center of his chest. "I don't know how far she threw me. I blacked out. When I came to, she was gone and then you were here."

Kaitlyn looked over his body and did not see any open wounds, scars, or blood. "I'm sure I'll have a giant bruise on my chest soon. Do I have one now?" Jerome attempted to unbutton his shirt but was unable to do so. Kaitlyn's fingers popped the buttons quickly. The triskelion medallion on his leather band necklace reflected the sun, creating a small pink light around it. A fist–sized red mark in the middle of his sternum was the only remnant of the attack.

"You look good. Holy crap. You're lucky."

Jerome coughed up a laugh. "I don't feel lucky." He coughed again. "I'll be okay." He again tried to get up. "We have to get out of here, Kaitlyn. This isn't normal."

"No. Stay down. I need to get Dr. Brungardt so he can look you over and make sure you're okay."

"I'm not an animal, Kait."

"He can still help with first aid and such."

"I'm serious. We need to get out of here. Cassie was too much. We can't stop her. There's nothing we can do. We need to go."

"We will. We'll go and get you help, but we still have to get Dr. Brungardt either way.

Jerome ignored this. "Just help me up."

"Stay down. I'll be right back, okay?" She stood, slapping at her pockets for her phone, but it was not there.

"What's wrong?"

"I left my phone in the Jeep. I'll just go find him."

She forced a smile. "I'll come right back for you. I promise. Whatever you do, don't move."

Kaitlyn grabbed a bottle of water from the back of the Jeep and found her phone. There were no new messages from Cathy, which Kaitlyn took to mean Cassie was still in the area. She found Dr. Thomas Brungardt in her contacts. She smiled as she realized she still had him saved as "T-Bag," as that's what Jerome liked to call him.

I'll change that later.

She pressed call and waited, looking out at the midday sun.

"Hey, you've reached Thomas. Leave a message and I'll call you back if I feel like it."

She hit call again, hoping for a different response, but it was the same message again.

Opening the text option, she tapped a message.

Kaitlyn: Need you ASAP. Jerome injured by Cassie. Straight west of Jeep.

She closed the phone and slid it into her pocket. She picked up the first aid kit. "I'll just do it myself." Her hand ran over her pocket to ensure the phone was there this time. She pulled back and closed the door when she heard someone yelling in the distance.

Brungardt?

A man stood in the back of a white pickup in the distance, shaking his fist and screaming obscenities. Two flags waved behind him from the siderails of the pickup. Kaitlyn remembered Cathy's text and knew instantly who was out there.

How did they find us? And how do they know that Cassie is here?

The man in the pickup stumbled. He half–climbed, half–fell out of the bed of the truck. Clumsily pulling himself up, he walked toward the trees. Kaitlyn locked eyes on the man's rifle and forgot all about the first aid kit. She reached into the truck and pulled out one of the rifles instead.

The more muscular man held Dr. Brungardt in a headlock of some sort. The guy next to him laughed, his beard bouncing with each heave of his chest. Kaitlyn looked down at the rifle in her hand and pulled it up. She aimed, but her tortuous breathes made it impossible to hold the gun in one place.

She considered just firing but did not want to hit

her friend. The man did not let go. Kaitlyn squeezed her eyes shut, counting down from ten to try to steady her shot.

Before she reached two, the taller of the men yelled, "I know you're out there! If you don't come out right now, I'm gonna blow this motherfucker's brains all over the place. Then I'm going to come find you."

With no choice, Kaitlyn quickly glanced around. She set the gun against a rock. She knew Nicolas would take it from her if he saw it, but if he did not know she had it, there was a chance she could get to it later if needed. Or so she told herself.

Kaitlyn took one deep breath and resigned herself to the fact there was no other way to save Dr. Brungardt. She stepped forward.

Samantha gave in. Nicolas had clearly said he knew she was out there. She walked out of the trees, but his back was to her. She followed Tobias' stare. Samantha's face fell as she saw another woman walk out of the trees, right where Nicolas was staring. The woman wore the same shirt as the man Nicolas was pointing his gun at. Samantha's cheeks blew outward as she let out a long breath.

She could not help these people, but this was her chance to get out of there.

Ready to run, Samantha turned around. She gasped audibly. The barrel of the gun was inches from her face.

She heard, "Bye, bitch."

Kaitlyn screamed as the gun went off.
Tobias and Nicolas turned, pulling their own weapons. Samantha's body thumped to the dirt; half of her head gone. Emmanuel lowered the weapon, blood running from his mangled arm.

"What? She started it."

Nicolas smirked, shaking his head, "What the fuck?" He pointed the gun at Dr. Brungardt, who had slipped away during the momentary distraction.

"Where the fuck do you think you're going?" Tobias held his weapon on Kaitlyn as he motioned for her to walk closer.

She stepped forward as Nicolas said, "Your boyfriend down here tells me that you have the tracker. Hand it over."

Brungardt spit out, "He's fucking lying." Nicolas' boot came down hard across the doctor's temple. Brungardt hit the dirt chin first, his tooth slicing his tongue.

"Get up!" Nicolas yelled. Dr. Brungardt didn't move. Nicolas poked him in the head with the rifle. At half the volume, Nicolas reiterated. "I said get up."

Brungardt pushed himself off the ground. Eye to eye with Nicolas, Dr. Brungardt's words ripped through his clenched teeth. "Go fuck yourself."

The warm wet brown goo splattered across Brungardt's left cheek, still warm and sticky. More coated the space between Tobias' two front teeth: a smile spreading wider. Brungardt swung hard, knowing he'd only get one chance. His fist connected with Tobias's lower jaw, almost correcting his overbite.

Nicolas laughed. "You kinda deserved that one." Brungardt swung at Nicolas. The second man easily dodged it, having known it was coming. "Wrong choice, asshole." The butt of his weapon drove directly into Brungardt's skull, only inches from where he'd been kicked a minute before.

Emmanuel raised his weapon in a quick motion, locking it directly on Kaitlyn's forehead. Nicolas bent down until he was able to look Brungardt in the eye. "You're done. You hear me? You pull that shit again, we put a bullet in your fuck buddy over here."

Nicolas gripped Brungardt's arms and pulled his wrists together, kneeling, pushing them into Brungardt's spine. He removed two zip ties from his pocket and wrapped the wrists together. Brungardt fought back at first, but Nicolas grabbed the doctor's hair by the roots, pulling his head up. The doctor saw Kaitlyn's bulging eyes, the sweat running down her face with her lurching breathing.

Be strong for her. Brungardt stopped struggling.

Nicolas pulled Dr. Brungardt to his feet and stood in front of him. "Now. Where the fuck is the bird? That's all I want. I want to put a single bullet in the bird's fucking heart and then I want to take her to the taxidermist and then home so my kids can ride her stupid stuffed body." He screamed in the doctor's face. "*Where the fuck is the bird?*"

"She's right behind you," Kaitlyn said.

Emmanuel didn't lower his weapon, but looked behind him, where Kaitlyn was pointing. The animal stood next to him. A low rumble roared through the area. Kaitlyn's teeth shook and her sternum vibrated.

"Now *this* is what I'm talking about!" Nicolas smiled.

The bird's head split Emmanuel's rib cage instantly. His heart was interrupted midbeat, popping as the beak ripped through it. The man was dead before his body crumpled to the ground, the gun in his hand luckily not firing. The other two men turned for cover, Nicolas already ducking behind a rock, tried to tell Tobias to do the same.

Brungardt locked eyes with Kaitlyn, "Get out of here!"

"No, we have to—"

The bird was airborne. It cleared eight and a half feet. Brungardt could not believe what he was seeing. Her wings spread out as she seemed to hover in the air, the glowing pink of her eyes illuminating everything around them even in the midday sun. He saw it before he felt it. The large talon opened his chest like an autopsy knife. The sting that followed didn't seem enough for the damage that had been done. The second talon scratched through Brungardt's face. The long middle claw caught his left eye and then the corner of his mouth, tearing the skin halfway down his neck.

He fell to the ground, face first. The beak ripped at his back, bite after bite. The small head shot down, severing Brungardt's spinal cord. Brungardt wanted to stand and run, but the world spun around him. The scent of roses was everywhere all at once and he smiled, even though his mouth no longer moved. He stared down with his remaining eye. The amount of blood pouring out of his chest onto the ground around him darkened. He wished he could tell his friend goodbye, but he could not see anything anymore.

He was still alive two minutes later when the bullets stopped but had no way to let anyone know.

Nicolas and Tobias unloaded on the bird.

Chapter Sixteen

The AR–15's each man carried were equipped with aftermarket magazines holding a hundred rounds each. The two men pulled their triggers repeatedly until both mags were empty. Feathers cascaded through the air, some coasting to the ground peacefully like whirlybirds in the early fall.

Cassie pulled her undersized wings toward her face, but it was not enough to protect her. Her large reptilian feet dug into the soil as round after round punctured her overgrown body.

When the bird finally hit the ground, Tobias still had shots left and emptied them as well.

"Not the head. Do not shoot the head!" Nicolas screamed, unsure if Tobias could hear him.

The men held their empty weapons as they each moved forward, eyes locked on the carcass in front of them. Nicolas' boot touched the deep black plumage of the bird's back. The bird did not move. He pushed against it harder, but there was still no response.

A warm glop of brown liquid shot from between Tobias' teeth, a perfect projectile bouncing off the ground as he moved toward the animal. The cassowary's legs were limp and extremely heavy. The grayish–white flesh appeared to have flecks of orange and blue now that Tobias was closer.

He grabbed what he considered to be the shin bone, his long fingers unable to completely encompass the leg bone, but it was the claw that held his attention.

The foot was tridactyl, the three toes pointing

wide in different directions. The scutes covering each created an armor over the toe resembling that of an armadillo.

Tobias pointed at the nine–inch long claw protruding from the middle toe. "I'll bet that would make a hell of a dagger."

"You can have it. You know I only want from here up." Nicolas' hand karate–chopped the cassowary's wattles as he said this. "Unless we're gonna grill it up. Then I might want some more."

Nicolas quickly drew a 9mm from his belt holster, cocking it, locked on Kaitlyn's back. "Where the fuck do you think you're going?"

She turned, slowly, her face red. "You got what you came for. You don't need to kill me."

"I don't want to kill you, lady. I just need your help."

"I'm not skinning her. It's bad enough that you—"

"What? Nobody said anything about skinning her. I just want you to take a picture. Do that and I'll let you walk right out of here. Same as you walked in." Nothing in Kaitlyn believed his words. Three humans and the bird lay dead around them. There was no reason to believe him. But Kaitlyn knew she did not have a choice. "Let's get it over with."

Tobias pointed to a more open area. "Should we move her over there?"

Nicolas stared at Tobias. "Are you stupid? She's gotta be a good two–twenty, numb nuts. I'm not dragging her over there. Get down here."

Nicolas drove both fists into the ground, adjusting his tailbone as he seated himself next to the bird. He propped the bird's head up, holding Cassie's dead body by the nape of the neck. "It's like Weekend at Birdie's!"

Tobias pulled a long suck of tobacco before

spitting it out. He positioned himself on the other side of Cassie. "Jesus Christ, man."

Kaitlyn motioned to Nicolas. "Phone?"

"That would help, huh?" Nicolas reached into his pocket, removed the phone and threw it to her. Kaitlyn lined up the shot, noticing there was no passcode on the screen. "Get like twenty of them. Just to be sure. You're shaking a lot."

Nicolas turned his attention to Cassie. "You should smile more. Why aren't you smiling?" Turning back, Nicolas threw his hands up. "What am I thinking? I've been saving this!" His fingers pulled the Marlboro box from his shirt pocket. The only cigarette inside sat upside down, the head facing the opening of the pack. Nicolas pulled it out with his teeth, flicked it around in his mouth and turned to Tobias. The lighter clicked three times before igniting the cigarette.

Nicolas inhaled deeply, breathed out, and smiled. "Cheese!"

As Kaitlyn hit the button, pink light burst from the cassowary with such force it burned both men like the July sun. Nicolas accidentally let go, shielding his eyes, "What the fuck was that?"

The light stopped midair. Kaitlyn watched it in wonder. It reversed, shooting back into the bird.

Tobias screamed. The cassowary stared him in the eyes. Her own eyes glowed bright pink. Her neck shot forward, her beak locking on either side of Tobias' beard. She pulled back, Tobias' lower jaw dislocating with the force. The left side hung from his mouth; the right side still holding on. A pool of brown liquid ran down his face and onto his shirt. Blood quickly replaced it.

The bird pulled back, the casque connecting with Nicolas' face, knocking him to the ground. The cassowary screamed, then clamped her mouth shut over Tobias' face. His body fell to the ground, half of his head was gone. The bird turned, spitting. A trail of dark red blood shot from the bird's mouth, muscle and tendon falling to the ground.

Nicolas pulled himself up to a sitting position, removing a 9mm from his shin holster. He fired it three times at close range. The bird pushed through what little pain resulted, propelling forward as one fights a heavy wind. Her neck bent forward, her small shoulders stiffened as she focused on her prey.

Mere inches from the bird, Nicolas' eyes never blinked. Spittle grew at the corner of his mouth, his corded neck throbbing with each breath. He focused solely on the need to dominate. He moved quickly, slamming his knife toward the bird's neck, but the pain in his own neck instantly screamed through his mind.

The bird's wings were open. The small claw on the right wing's second digit was embedded in the skin of Nicolas' neck. The bird lifted him off the ground by just the hook. Nicolas' feet swung back and forth in the air as the bird watched. The claw was out as quickly as it went in. Nicolas slammed into the ground, crumpling on his own stomach. As he tried to push himself up, the bird took two steps forward, standing directly on his back.

The large animal stood for a second, preening her black plumage, possibly cleaning the blood off her wings and back. Nicolas endured the pain of the massive cassowary's full weight, his breathing sporadic at best. The two reptilian claws pushed off with all their power as the bird lifted straight into the air above him. Tears escaped as Nicolas gasped for air.

The cassowary dropped; the impact shattered three of Nicolas' vertebrae. His arm went numb. He could not move his fingers, but in that moment he did not even try.

Cassie pulled her leg behind her. The middle

toe's nail was now a full foot long. The bird drove it straight through Nicolas' perineum. The bird pulled it out and kicked him the same way several more times until there was nothing left but a mash of flesh and blood. The cassowary pulled back, head tilted, watching Nicolas bleed out. She had no intention of finishing the job quickly.

Kaitlyn's miscalculation was a large one. She had come to believe she knew these animals. She trusted them. She thought knowing their stereotypical behavior on any given day somehow made her safe. It was only standing in that clearing in the trees that she realized that had all been in her head.

She looked around and saw a million exit routes, but each one of them ended with her being skewered by the beast towering in front of her. None of the scenarios in her head ended with the bird giving her a pass because Kaitlyn was a good zookeeper. Cassie was gone. The monstrosity that in front of Kaitlyn was not the bird she had loved.

The bird stretched. It was impossible, but the cassowary stood seven–and–a–half feet tall, more than two feet taller than she had at the zoo. Her eyes shown bright pink. The violets, blues, and reds of the double wattle darkened and lightened, throbbing with each heartbeat. The blood soaked claws on her talons were three times as long as they should have been. Her casque was thicker, taller than ever before.

"What happened to you?" Kaitlyn stared into the pink light emanating from the bird's eyes. "You died. You fucking died. And you're back. *Again.*"

It was the last word that ripped at Kaitlyn. She had seen it on the drone footage, when it made no sense. Then she saw it again a few feet in front of her. And yet, there was no way to believe it. Kaitlyn released a long breath.

Cassie's beak shot forward.

Pink light enveloped everything around her as Kaitlyn squeezed her eyes shut and tucked her chin into her shoulder. She braced herself for the pain, no matter how quickly it devoured her.

But none came.

She stood in that position for an eternity. Or maybe two seconds. Time all felt the same to Kaitlyn. The sun shone warm and calm through the shadows of the leaves. Shuffling back a step or two, she opened her eyes and found only an empty clearing. Kaitlyn's palms rubbed her eyes before sliding over her gaping mouth. She let out one long, purposeful breath as she scanned the area, but she knew in her heart that Cassie was no longer there.

Kaitlyn called the police, trying to explain to emergency services where they would find the bodies and that she had the photographs to prove her story.

Kaitlyn knelt next to Dr. Brungardt's body and mumbled a very quick prayer. "I'm sorry I couldn't save you." As she walked away, Thomas Brungardt's phone rang. Two rings later, Kaitlyn grabbed it from the ground near Tobias.

The screen read, "CRAZY UNCLE KEVIN."

She slid the bar to green and tried to audibly say hello.

"Thomas? That you? Is J. Michael with you?"

"It's... it's Kaitlyn, Mr. Lewis."

"Kaitlyn! Great. Is J. Michael there? He just called me and—"

He's alive. That was her first thought. *Jerome was alive.*

"He sounded real upset. Where are you guys? Is he with you and Thomas?"

Her face tightened as she looked back at Dr. Brungardt's body. "I don't know where he is. I had to leave him after he was attacked. I'm heading back now."

"Attacked? What do you mean?"

As she walked, Kaitlyn attempted to explain everything to Kevin, but it was hard to focus. The story made less sense coming out of her mouth than the reality did.

Kevin eventually cut her off. "I just saw her on Twitter. The bird's been spotted at West Gate. I'm heading over there. You guys meet me in the parking lot." He hung up before she could say more.

West Gate? The mall was less than a mile from her. Her throat hitched as Kaitlyn stared at the empty clearing where she had left Jerome. She raced along the same trail she had taken less than thirty minutes before, but she already knew she would not find the Jeep when she got there.

CHAPTER SEVENTEEN

Kaitlyn trudged back to the clearing, opting to wait for the police. As much as she wanted to help capture Cassie, there was nothing she could do. She could not walk the mile to the mall. Even if she did, Cassie was beyond the point where they could bring her back to the Preserve and wait for this to blow over. *I'm better off just staying here*, she told herself.

Her fingers instinctively grabbed her phone. Opening Facebook Messenger, she saw the green dot next to Jerome's thumbnail. He was online. She pushed the video chat option.

You better fucking answer.

The video buffered and loaded. Jerome sat in the driver's seat. The Jeep did not appear to be moving. "Kaitlyn?"

"Where the fuck are you?"

"I didn't know you made it. I wouldn't have left you."

"What the hell do you mean?"

"I thought Cassie got you, too. After what she did to Thomas—"

Kaitlyn's left eye closed as her tongue pushed against her bottom teeth. "What are you saying? How do you know about that? Did you see what happened to us?

Jerome swallowed hard, looking out the passenger window and then back at the phone. "I mean... I walked out to find you. And I saw it. I saw her kill that cowboy looking dude. I saw her... eat Thomas."

"What? Why didn't you help us?"

"I thought it was too late. I ran to safety."

Kaitlyn tried to digest what he'd said.

"How did you do that? How is that possible" She finally said. "With your injuries?" She paused, waiting for the pain. Something told her she knew the answer, but Kaitlyn needed to hear it. "Tell me the truth, Jerome."

It came easier than she had expected. It helped that he did not bother lying. His lips pursed together. His hands cut the air with choppy movements as he spoke; but he was truthful. "I wasn't attacked. I just... I thought if you thought I was hurt we could give up. We could go back to the Preserve. Let the authorities end this. Do you get how dangerous she is?"

"I saw how dangerous she was. Up close. Apparently you saw it too and then you ran the other direction."

"I didn't know it would be like this!" His own scream devolved into blubbering.

"What did you think it would be like, Jerome?"

"I thought we'd go find her together. We could have an adventure together. We'd put her in the trailer and come back and then go celebrate together. Now that you and Ryan broke up, I just—"

Kaitlyn's own eyes might as well have shot pink rays. "Are you fucking serious right now?"

"I thought if I could stop her... If I could save everyone. You'd give me a chance." He shook his head as Kaitlyn glared into the distance. "That's probably not even true. I knew what she was. We all saw what she did to Michael. I knew I'd have to put her down. I thought you'd see me as a hero."

"I don't even know who the fuck you are right now." Kaitlyn fell into a seated position, landing on a large rock only twenty feet from the little that remained of Nicolas' body.

Jerome's words seemed far away, but it was her own inability to stay grounded in them. "Look, you just... you don't understand. I need to tell you everything, you're probably not going to believe most of it, even with what you've seen. I'm sure it started hundreds of years ago, but my knowledge only goes to the things Grandma told me and the stuff I was able to find online in the last couple of months."

"What the hell are you talking about? Can you get to the point?"

"I'm getting there!" His words spit out of his mouth. The anger seething forth was harder and harder to hold back. But he tried. He inhaled deeply, closing his eyes. He pulled the triskelion medallion out of his shirt into view of the camera. The silver metal stood in sharp contrast to his black zoo Security shirt. The braided leather band pulled at the nape of Jerome's neck as he held the triskelion out toward Kaitlyn.

"It's all this thing. This is what caused it. This isn't the original chain. That one is buried six feet under with my grandmother. I bought a cheap imitation at a store in the mall and switched them out before the wake."

He stared at the floor, rubbing his palm against his teary eye. "I've never said it out loud before. It hurts more than I expected." Jerome shifted in his seat as he readied to continue. Kaitlyn stared in silence. Jerome gauged her reactions before deciding to continue.

"The first time I saw Majerle die—"

"The first time?" Kaitlyn's eyes grew.

His cadence iced over. "Can you let me fucking talk? It's going to get weirder than that. Just let me do this, please. I gotta get this all out at once."

He took a deep breath and began, not looking directly at the phone's camera lens. "The first time I saw Majerle die was the fourth time he died. At the time he was already almost twenty–five pounds. He lay there in the street. The Honda Civic that hit him just kept going. They didn't even slow down to see what they'd hit. Majerle wasn't breathing. He just lay there, tire treads down his center.

"I got closer and closer. Not because I was upset. He was mean as fuck. I was glad he was dead... for the minute or so that he was. But as I checked on him, it happened. Pink light, blinding pink light, shot out of him. It turned around in midair. Or whatever you would call it. It's fucking light. You know? But then it all went back into him. He... reinflated or some shit. Sat right up. I swear he was bigger than before he got hit. Like that light overfilled him or something. He licked his paw twice and then stretched out like any house cat getting up from a nap, kneading the pavement, ass in the air.

"Majerle walked over to me and then swiped at me. His trimmed nails were already long and sharp again, cutting my skin and leaving track marks down my forearm not unlike the marks on the back half of his body from that Civic."

Jerome tugged on the triskelion medallion. "I know you saw Cassie do the same thing. I know because when it happens, this thing also lights up." His head hung. "That's what I'm telling you. It's the necklace's fault."

"And who used it?"

"Oh, fuck off. Cassie was very sick. I saved her. For you." He paused. The mere mention of the bird's name had elicited a reaction. Jerome tried to suppress a smile. "I was trying to help her. I made my way through the Preserve for my normal walkthrough, like I do every night. My first trip near her enclosure, I knew she wasn't doing well. Her breath was soft and slow but looked like it hurt. The second time, she was lying on her side. I came up the safety passage near the fence line and entered. I wouldn't normally have done so, but I really thought she was already dead. She wasn't, but she couldn't put up a fight if she wanted to.

"Thomas told me she'd been losing weight, but I wasn't prepared for how small she looked up close. She was barely breathing. She couldn't stand. She tried as I came closer, but she didn't even get off the ground. Her foot just pushing into the dirt and kicking it behind her. I didn't know what to do, so I went to call Thomas, but before I did, I decided to take pictures to send him. As I did, Cassie raised her head and looked at me. The brown around her eyes was dim. Not at all like it looked in the past.

"That's when I thought about Majerle. I'd seen the same look in his eyes the time he actually died of old age. Sure, part of it was the cloudy eye that cats get, but it was also just a dimming of the light. Like the soul fading. That's what I saw when I looked at Cassie. She was giving up.

"I leaned in. I was so close I could smell the wet feathers sticking together. She gargled. Loud. Skin folds all bouncing on her throat. Then it all just stopped."

His words hung on the air as Kaitlyn took them in. He stared, waiting for her to say something, but she did not. Jerome nodded, "She died, Kaitlyn. She died right in front of me and there was nothing I could do."

"You could've left her alone. Let her die in peace."

Jerome continued as though Kaitlyn hadn't spoken. "Pink light flooded everything around me. Staring down, I realized it was resonating from this medallion. I'd heard the stories about Majerle and I'd seen it happen once or twice, but I didn't know how to control it. I couldn't purposely do it. And it flooded into Cassie. That fucking bird was dead, Kaitlyn. Dead. And now it was sitting up, looking at me. Watching me as I took more and more steps backward."

"She."

"What?"

"She. You said 'it'. Cassie's a she."

"Sure. Sorry. Whatever. And then its eyes. Sorry. *Her* eyes. Bright light shot out of them like lasers. I ran as quickly as I could. She didn't follow, but I didn't have time to even think about that. I just ran. I ran down the safety paths and out the holding cell door. I hit the codes to lock everything and finally looked back.

"And I saw Michael Flanders and I didn't do anything, Kaitlyn. I didn't warn him. I didn't want anyone to know. And what would I have said anyway? How do you explain to someone that you made a fucking zombie cassowary? He wouldn't have believed me. He hated me and didn't want me anywhere near the birds as it was."

Or you, he did not add aloud.

Kaitlyn's open palm tapped the rock she sat on, as she squinted into the sun, wondering how much longer the police would take. "Why did you run away from Dr. Brungardt instead of maybe using it to help him?"

Jerome softened, his body relaxing a bit as he lost himself in his memories. "It doesn't work on humans. They tried it on my father when his pancreatic cancer got really bad."

"Why did it not bring Majerle back to life the last time?"

"When Grandma died, the medallion was with her at the funeral home in Glendale. Kevin took Majerle all the way out to Mesa. Majerle knew something was wrong when she didn't come back. He just gave up and crawled into a cabinet in the bathroom and died. I guess maybe the medallion was far enough away from him that it didn't bring him back... or he chose not to. How should I know?"

"Cassie won't make that choice. So that just leaves you. Just don't go anywhere near her. We know where she is right now. You just have to drive far enough away from her."

A smile spread across his face. "Come on, Kaitlyn. You know it's too late for that. There's only one way for this to end." He grabbed his rifle from the passenger seat. "It's been fun catching up, but I gotta run. I have a hot date with a crazy chick."

Kaitlyn stared at her phone for almost a full minute after the call ended.

As she listened to the sirens in the distance, Kaitlyn watched the flags waving in the wind, each haphazardly propped at a different angle from the sides of the pickup.

Nicolas seemed like the kind of guy who always had to be in control, so she assumed the keys were in his pockets. The mutilated flesh had seemingly become one with the denim of his Wranglers. She did not want to touch him at all, but she knelt down, turning away as she thrust her hand into his right pocket as her throat buckled and she dry heaved twice before fully vomiting. As her fingers found the Dallas Cowboys key ring, she wiped her clean sleeve across her mouth and walked toward the truck.

CHAPTER EIGHTEEN

Tasha Van Kleek walked hand in hand with her daughter, Landry. Tasha looked around at the choices of places to eat.

"Pizza sounds good... but they have excellent Bar–B–Q over there..." Her eyebrow raised. "Oh my god. That place has fresh donuts!" Her attention immediately went to a man carrying a container from a nearby food truck. "What does he have?"

The man smiled, "Wings! Double battered. Super crunchy!" He kept walking as Tasha plotted ways to steal his food.

Meanwhile Landry stared straight ahead at Cassie and the bird stared right back at her.

"Mommy, look at the bird."

Tasha was not looking at a full bird, but she could not take her eyes off the turkey drumstick wrapped in bacon a lady near the splashpad was eating. There were almost three hundred people at West Gate Mall and it was starting to feel to Tasha like eighty percent of the them had food and she did not.

"What's that, hon?"

"Look at the pretty bird."

Tasha glanced at her phone's notification as she mumbled an "Uh–huh."

"Is he a boy a girl?"

Tasha looked up. Her mouth fell open, as her head jerked back. A small gasp escaped as her footing stumbled. She had seen this bird all over social media. She had made jokes about it and shared memes. And now it was staring right at her daughter. There was a noticeable rise in the pitch of her voice as she said, "Come here."

Tasha pulled Landry into her arms as she backed away from the cassowary. The small bag of random purchases from the candy store knocked against her thigh as it dangled from her wrist. A coldness hit her core. Her breath hitched as she said, "It's okay, Landry. Let's go this way."

Tasha took another step back. The bird's head tilted, her eyes still had not left Landry. Tasha steadied her foot as she moved backward again, almost to the corner of the sushi store next to them.

Ooh. Sushi.

The bird's head shot sideways, focusing on two teenage girls as they ran up, phones out, pointed at the bird, "That's the one!" The girl in the green dress screamed. "Hashtag it!"

"We're going to get so many likes!" yelled the other.

Tasha turned the corner, moving quickly. As the laughter of the teen girls became screams and more screams joined in, she scooped Landry into her arms and increased her speed, just hoping to make it to her car in time.

Thirty seconds earlier, Hunter Womack turned to Liz Hansen and muttered, "You're sure?"

Liz smiled, holding her phone out. The screen showed the cassowary resting comfortably on a bed of tulips on the side of a clothing store in West Gate Mall. "She's here. See? Twitter can be useful."

"I suppose. Let's get the stuff."

He reached back for the microphone and the stand. Liz carried the camera. As the back doors of the CHANNEL 3 EYEWITNESS NEWS doors closed, the screaming began.

"This is it! Let's go," screamed Liz as the two ran from the parking lot into the mall area, having no idea they were less than a hundred feet from the beginning of Cassie's rampage.

As she turned the corner, Liz's soles squealed against the concrete, grinding to a stop. "Hunter, look out!"

A pink light overtook everything around him as the bird's beak shot toward his chest. Hunter's weight shifted to the right as he curved his way from the animal.

Cassie took another shot, her mouth wide, repeated grunts pouring from within. The beak clamped down, biting the middle of the boom mic stand Hunter wielded between his hands. He pushed back at Cassie, sure that the boom pole would bend under the pressure, but it did not. The bird let go and shook her head side to side.

Hunter pulled the mic stand back, ready to swing it like a baseball bat.

"Alright, you archaic dinosaur wannabe! Listen up! You see this? This... is my boom pole," he yelled. "You can find one in a lot of electronic goods departments. This sweet baby right here was made in China, probably. Retails for about three hundred bucks. It's got durable lightweight, carbon fiber, a built—in internal XLR cable, soft, comfortable padding on the handle and—"

Hunter stared at the bird as he squared up his swing and pulled back. "Best of all, it's got—"

His eyes grew wide. The casque protruded out of his back for a mere second before Cassie pulled it through the front again. Hunter's body collapsed to the ground, the boom pole rattling on the pavement beside him. Liz dropped the camera and ran for her life.

Cassie turned the other way and ran straight for

a large group of people, still in shock over what they had just witnessed.

The security cameras did not catch the actual deaths of the teenage girls taking selfies with the bird or what happened to Hunter Womack, but the majority of the rampage was pieced together later from mall security footage and eventually leaked onto YouTube.

Cassie ran through the crowd of people gathered for that night's hockey game. Some flew through the air as she kicked them, slammed her neck into them, or, in one case, pushed a guy out of the way with a butt bump.

A close up shot showed a couple who narrowly missed being attacked giggling nervously about it until Cassie came back through and drove her beak through the woman's head, her FroYo falling from her hand, spilling to the ground. The man she was with ran, but Cassie's talons found him before long.

A small child playing on the splashpad was scooped up as Cassie wrapped her neck around the girl like an elephant's trunk. The girl went airborne. When they found her, it took a few minutes to figure out what they were looking at.

Several people ran into the HEY, BATTER, BATTER hot wing food truck, believing they would be safe there, but Cassie ripped the side of the truck open like a tin can. One woman's head was still in the deep fryer when authorities arrived.

Cassie simply stampeded through others, crushing them under her feet, her claws ripping in and out of people. She shook one free of her foot while impaling another with her beak. She tipped a car on top of someone hiding behind it. Another was thrown through a clothing shop.

One girl slammed into the candy store, her

neck breaking before she hit the ground.

When she grew bored, Cassie simply stopped and lay down. All told, over forty people were killed and another thirty survived with various injuries.

Jerome stood like a sole survivor looking out on a wasted battlefield. He inhaled the dust hanging in the air as he surveyed the damage. Broken blinds fluttered in a shattered insurance office window; a man's body draped over a smashed cubicle. His feet had tipped a filing cabinet. Up above, a wrenching screech of grinding metal escaped as a section of the upper walkway dangled, tearing away from the building.

He stepped forward, his boot catching in a small gap where pavement was torn lose. Cracks ran across the sidewalks and into the roadways. One ran to a parked car, smashed and flipped on its side. The headlights were still on. A piece of fabric waved in the wind like a flag of surrender; a white shirt from someone who did not get out of the way in time.

The candy store where Tasha Van Kleek had been less than twenty minutes before lay destroyed; the fabric awning ripped away from the entrance. Chunks of the building's façade were broken away and cracks spiderwebbed through the remains. The decorative building columns were snapped in half as a teenage girl went through them. Her corpse lay crumpled against the corner of the building, her half–eaten chocolate melting in the Arizona sun.

One food truck had been torn open. In the other, food continued to burn on the grill, abandoned in the moment as the men and women inside ran in terror. The burnt smell mixed with the acrid, chemical–laden smoke filling the air around him. Jerome stepped over branches lying in the street, some mangled by falling rubble. The water in the splashpad had turned murky, polluted by the debris. Jerome was numb, touching things without even feeling them as he made his way toward Cassie.

Two flags blew in the wind behind her as the tires squealed during the turn. Kaitlyn did not slow down. The raised wheels jumped the curb pulling into the parking lot. The cab shook as Kaitlyn straightened out the wheel. The cooler sloshed in the bed as she took the final turn and screeched to a stop.

Kevin stood next to his car, parked haphazardly on the sidewalk next to Johnny Rockets. He waved one arm in the air, his ball cap in his hand. As her feet hit the pavement, Kaitlyn smiled, "How did you know it was me?"

Kevin shrugged. "I didn't. But I figured whoever was behind the wheel was the kind of person who could help me out."

Kevin removed a Browning AB3 300WSM from his trunk and handed it to Kaitlyn. "Thirty cal. This baby never fails me when I'm picking off javelinas on the back eighty." He paused. "Not that we have eighty. But you know what I mean. This will stop the bird."

"I can't use this."

Kevin sighed. "Look, you're gonna have to get over your fear of guns or refusal to shoot 'em or whatever we're working with here. We're not going to get many shots at this and I need you to at least try."

"I don't have a fear of guns. I fly back to South Dakota and hunt with my dad every year. I can't use this because guns don't work."

Kevin laughed. "Well hot damn. If that's the issue, good news. Guns will work just fine. They already have. Repeatedly. That medallion is the issue. We gotta get it away from J. Michael and break it."

Kaitlyn opened the chamber and dropped bullets in. "Let's go."

The bird raised her head, staring straight at Jerome. A buzz of adrenaline coursed through his body. The dust in the air held the pink blaze of the beast's eyes. She was taller, wider. Her feet looked twice as big as they had at the Preserve, but Jerome had no way to know for sure.

He paused, feeling safe in the knowledge that she wouldn't attack him any more than Majerle had ever bitten his grandmother. He removed the triskelion medallion from his shirt, let it hang in the open where Cassie could see it. As soon as he did, the bird lowered her head almost in reverence.

Jerome moved closer, "Look at us. What a fucking pair. You were supposed to help me get the girl. You're my wingman!" A smirk slid across his lips as he held his hand out, palm down. "*Wing*... never mind." Cassie rubbed against his outstretched palm the same way Majerle had. The bird's keratin casque was warm to the touch. Jerome smiled, "But it's okay. I'm going out the hero. I'll be banging so many chicks I won't give a shit what a bitch Kaitlyn turned out to be."

His thumb and index finger gripped the medallion. "*Back*!" Jerome bellowed. The bird took three steps back, mesmerized. Her tridactyl feet planted into the ground as the rest of her muscles relaxed. Jerome took two steps back himself and raised the rifle, locking in directly on Cassie's chest.

Kaitlyn's voice commanded the air around her. "Jerome! No!"

His eyes grew. He did not turn right away, breathing in and out forcefully as he finally turned. "Kaitlyn! Stay back! I got this!"

Kevin's voice boomed. "Drop it, J. Michael. I don't want to light you up, but if I do, you're not coming back like that creature does."

Jerome's eyes darted from the bird to Kevin and

back again. "Back off and let me handle this."

"We know it was you, J. Michael. Put the gun down."

Jerome slowly lowered his weapon, placing it on the ground in front of him. His fingers slid to the triskelion. Staring deep into the cassowary's pink eyes.

Kaitlyn instinctively pulled the trigger. The bullet ripped through Jerome's forearm and cut across his stomach. He stumbled forward, staring at Kaitlyn in the final seconds.

He screamed. "I gave everything for you, you piece of shit. Fucking bitch!" Pointing the rifle at Kaitlyn, Jerome winced in pain as his arm throbbed. He tried to steady his shot.

The bird was fast. So fast. Her head shot straight up and then forward. The beak smashed through the middle of Jerome's chest. His sternum exploded. His heart stopped almost instantly. His finger fell away from the trigger as his body collapsed to the ground.

Pink light exited around Jerome's body, dissipating in the air. On his shirt lay the shattered remains of the triskelion, the middle missing entirely, the silver outer circle destroyed.

Kevin pulled the trigger several times in quick succession as he ran at the bird. The flesh of the animal's left leg exploded as the bullets ripped four holes in it. The bird turned away, unable to run.

Kevin jumped, his fingers gripped the coarse feathers of the bird. He had a choice to make and made one he never thought he would even consider. The gun dropped to the ground as Kevin reached up for the next handful of feathers. Then another. As he mounted the bird, Cassie hitched and bucked. She threw her neck back, missing Kevin by less than an inch. She tried again and again, to no avail.

Kaitlyn trembled, the gun in her hand moving

too much to take a clear shot. She pictured pulling the trigger, the bird bucking, the bullet hitting Kevin. Inhaling deeply, Kaitlyn tried to refocus, knowing she might be the only one who could put an end to this.

Kevin concentrated on Cassie's neck. He ignored her actual head and focused on the tough blue scaly skin running to her body instead. Soon, he saw not the neck of a cassowary but a ring–necked snake with bluish–gray dorsal coloration, running down not to bright pink wattles but to vivid ventral shades.

Kevin watched the faux snake move and learned its rhythm without much effort. His hands shot out, as they had a hundred times before, and gripped the monster with both fists, smiling like he had caught the biggest snake he had ever seen.

The bird's range of motion limited, she still found a way to peck at Kevin's right arm, the only thing she could reach. The beak nipped at the skin, repeatedly, the bites ripping at the angel tattooed on his forearm. Kevin squeezed his eyes, trying to ignore the pain as his flexor snapped and rolled up on itself. He instantly lost grip. He right arm hung useless. He did not let go of the left, gripping the bird's neck and turning it toward him. He brought his foot up, driving his boot into the other side of the animal's neck.

The cassowary's head spun the opposite direction. The crunch of bones echoed as vertebrae shattered and the bird dropped.

Kevin came to with his cheek scraped against gritty pavement. Pain splintered throughout so many parts of his body he could only suck in a gasp of air before it hurt too much to breathe. He did not need a medical degree to know something inside was broken. Cassie lay some fourteen feet away. Her own breath hitched as she stared at him. The pink light in her eyes was gone, a trail of blood ran from her beak. Two feet were planted next to Cassie's head. Kevin looked up and saw Kaitlyn standing there.

Kaitlyn closed her eyes and said a quick prayer over Cassie.

She pulled the trigger.

Chapter Nineteen

The chalky, thick dust in Kaitlyn's mouth curdled at the touch of her tongue. She spit on the pavement and turned away from the animal she had put down. Her heels echoed as she walked to Kevin and laid the gun next to him.

She did not wait for anything he had to say. In that moment, she had no desire to stay connected to anything around her. She turned and walked away from him.

Liz Hansen was beyond nervous. Her fingers clicked her phone screen and opened incorrect apps as she tried to pull up her voice recorder. Kaitlyn was getting closer. She could not miss her chance.

This is it, Liz. This is your Dan Rather tells the world about Kennedy moment.

Kaitlyn stomped by at impressive speed, but Liz was ready for her. "Ma'am. Can I get a second?"

"Not right now."

"I'm Liz, Liz Hansen. Channel 3 Eyewitness News. I gotta get this story."

"So, go get it. Your story is in there," Kaitlyn, called, walking backward, pointing back at the most damaged section of the mall.

"But don't you get it?" Liz said, "You're a hero!"

Kaitlyn stopped, turned, and stared at Liz, but didn't say anything.

Liz swallowed hard. "You're a fucking hero, lady! I can already see the headline: Good Girl With

GUN! You're going to be a legend."

Kaitlyn said nothing, as she took several more steps.

"Where are you going? I'm trying to tell the world how important you are. What a hero you are." Liz threw her arms open. "I'm trying to empower you! And you're just going to walk away from that?"

Kaitlyn turned, she held eye contact, even as her eyebrows squished in a glare. "Empower me?"

"Yeah. Once we share your story, you'll—"

"My story?"

"Yes!"

"Then shouldn't I be the one to tell it?"

"Yes! Absolutely!" Liz smiled as she looked down at her phone and started the voice recorder. "Okay, here we go. This is Liz Hansen, and I'm here with... um... please state your name for the record"

Liz looked up.

Kaitlyn was gone.

Eight weeks passed before Kaitlyn saw Kevin Lewis again.

"You made it! I'm so glad!" Kaitlyn's smile beamed as Kevin walked toward her.

He held out his hand to shake hers. "Great to see you too, kid."

"What are you doing? We're huggers here." She leaned in, hugging Kevin. "Not really. Don't try hugging the other keepers."

"So, is it here?" Kevin looked both directions. His eyes locked on the bird walking toward them. "Oh shit."

"Oh, that's Casey." Kaitlyn said, watching as the male cassowary paced the enclosure that once belonged to Cassie. Kaitlyn smiled. "He's harmless." She shrugged. "Probably."

Two men walked toward them. One pulled a cart

behind him with a wooden park bench on it. Kevin took his hat off, holding it to his chest. "Oh, wow. It's beautiful."

He watched in silence as the men bolted the bench to the ground. Over and over, he read the words etched into the wood;

In Loving Memory of Michael Flanders, who spent his happiest hours watching the cassowaries.

Kevin didn't look directly at Kaitlyn, but her occasional sniffles told him she was fighting back tears. "I sure wish I could've met him."

As soon as the installation was complete, the man who appeared to be in charge stood, tipped his hat to Kaitlyn, and said, "We'll meet you over there." He turned and left. Kaitlyn ran her hand across the name Michael Flanders one time, smiling lightly to herself.

As they walked, Kevin said, "It took me a long time to realize the real reason J. Michael was so intent on me helping finding Cassie was because of mom's triskelion medallion. I had no idea. With mom in the ground, when I found Majerle dead under the bathroom sink, I thought all that shit was behind us. I thought the damn thing was just too far away to raise the demon cat again. I didn't realize till I saw that drone footage on Twitter.

"When I saw the pink light and the bird raise up and attack those cops... I knew there was only one way animals get that pink light. And there was only one other person who could have had the relic and known what to do with it."

He looked down. "I would give anything to go back and stop it. Save your friends."

Kaitlyn put an arm on his shoulder. "You can't blame yourself. It wasn't you."

Passing the kangaroo exhibit, Kevin watched the large Red eat grass. He appeared to be the only male in the enclosure, although Kevin could not be sure. He was a beautiful creature and watching him for a second, Kevin felt completely at peace.

They stood in silence for a while watching the White Tail Deer. Kevin finally broke the silence with a smile. "You know, back in Rockbridge, we used to hunt these things. They sure are tasty."

Kaitlyn punched him in the arm. "Come on."

The two reached the nocturnal animals building. It made Kevin slightly uncomfortable to have a woman hold the door for him, but he went in anyway. He stopped for a full minute watching the possums. The larger one rolled on the dirt in the enclosure, its dirty white fur bristled as it growled in Kevin's direction. "They're certainly not the friendliest." Kaitlyn said.

Kevin followed behind her as they reached the exhibit which had been Dr. Brungardt's favorite. "He spent a lot of time here," Kaitlyn said.

"Oh yeah. I always watched his YouTube show where he'd teach the kids about the animals. I love his series, '*Chilling with The 'Dillo*!' And all the videos of these guys messing with each other, rolling up into balls and whatnot. Or when we'd see how crazy their claws are."

The two went silent as the memorial bench arrived.

As Kevin read, IN LOVING MEMORY OF DR. THOMAS BRUNGARDT, he smiled to Kaitlyn. "He was like another nephew. Him and J. Michael spent so much time together the last few years. He always said he'd do anything for us." His smile faded. "And Jerome paid him back like this."

Kevin fought his tears successfully but would spend ten minutes alone crying in his truck after he left the Preserve. He snapped several pictures of the name piece. "Sorry. I don't know when I'll make it back here again."

"Your name is on the list. You have a free membership for life."

Kevin started to sit down and stopped. "Wait. Is it acceptable to sit on these?"

"Of course. That's what they're for. It's a place to share something a loved one enjoyed even after they're gone. And we all loved Dr. Brungardt very much."

The two of them sat listening to Dr. Brungardt's videos as they watched the armadillos run around, bouncing off of one another.

Kaitlyn smiled, "What a life. Sometimes it's hard to think of any other animal as laid back and happy as the 'dillo."

Kevin smiled. "Maybe a cobra."

ACKNOWLEDGEMENTS

I put out a call to my friends to see who would let me kill them in this book. I thought it would simply be fun to write in a bunch of the people who make my daily life better in the same manner that Alan Baxter wrote in many of the authors involved in the original Twitter conversation.

While there are some fun in–jokes with the people listed in this book (including a long Army of Darkness reference that probably doesn't overly fit in the story) they are still very fictionalized versions of themselves and in real life, many of them are nothing at all like the characters portrayed in this story.

I am in debt to each of them for, in some way, helping me deal with the depression, self–doubt, and lack of desire to create that I have experienced during COVID–19. The people I've written into this book are often the same people who provide reasons to smile and support for my writing career.

They mean the world to me.

Thank you to the following people:

Lynda, my wife, for putting up with the weirdness of living with a writer and the strange questions I ask every 10 minutes or so.

Alan Baxter	Kealan Patrick Burke
Stephanie Rabig	Sean Seebach
Max Booth III	Donald R. Guillory
John C. Wilson	Jared Sage
Jackie Mojica	Vincent V. Cava
Michael Flanders	John Chole
Cathy Cakebread	Jerome McClintock
Thomas Brungardt	Kaitlyn Lenhart
Adam Goldman	Andy Winters
Kevin Lewis *aka* Crank	Alayna Amaro
Allie Jo Thompson	Tyler J. Reilly
Fernando Ramos	AJ Hernandez
Allison Lovecraft	Ian Lovecraft
Hunter Womack	Shelly Grant
Brian Haas	Samantha Langdon
Tasha Van Kleek	Landry Luckett
Laurel Hightower	Gemma Amor
Bracken MacLeod	Mikayla Van de Berg
Mike Stevens	Vanessa Gorden
Aine Leicht	Diana Ramsden

And *Bowling For Soup*, because that's all I listened to while writing this book.

ZERO: LANCASTER'S GREATEST SUPERHERO
Horror 2018

Since 1985, over 500 overweight teenagers have come to Camp Wašíču, looking to lose weight, gain self-confidence, and turn their lives around.

Phillip McCracken arrives, weighing in at almost 400 pounds; but the baggage he carries from the past affects him much more deeply than the numbers of the scale. When a homicidal maniac hell-bent on revenge attacks, Phillip will be forced to either find the courage to save the people around him or fall victim to his own self-doubt.

Or possibly a machete.

Filled with allusions to the Slasher films of yesteryear, Fat Camp delivers horror, humor, and a little slice of nostalgia for anyone who grew up even slightly afraid of the dark.

If you enjoyed this book, please consider leaving a review. All reviews help the book get into more hands, and more sales results in more donations and hopefully more cassowary lives are saved.

They really are beautiful creatures and I've come to love them very much. So please help us out and take two minutes to leave a few words on any review site.

Thank you.

Something is wrong in the small outback town of Morgan Creek. A farmer goes missing after a blue in the pub. A teenage couple fail to show up for work. When Patrick and Sheila McDonough investigate, they discover the missing persons list is growing. Before they realize what's happening, the residents of the remote town find themselves in a fight for their lives against a foe they would never have suspected. And the dry red earth will run with blood.

Abigail Laine is comfortable being the sheriff of Rockbridge, Ohio. She only conducts a few traffic stops a week, has minimal paperwork, and cruises the town's mostly vacant streets. She has plenty of time to read and keep her living space and work area orderly. But when Caleb Welsh is murdered on his way home late one Friday night, Abigail is forced to blow the dust off her badge and find the killer.

With the help of Rockbridge's finest civilians, Laine must draw a line in the salt lick and assure that The Buck Stops Here.

THe NecRONOMi.COM

About The Author

James Sabata is a comedic horror author, screenwriter, and co-host of TheNecronomi.Com podcast.

James has written four novels, two novellas, and so many rejected screenplays he can use the pages to stay warm all winter.

Which hasn't really been an issue since the father of four lives in Phoenix, Arizona.

Find him online at:
Twitter - @JamesSabata
Twitter - @TheNecronomi
Facebook - @JamesSabataAuthor
Instagram - @JamesSabataAuthor

To find more photos of James, please check the walls of your local post office.